THE BEGINNING OF THE END

A Christian Speculative Fiction

LORANA HOOPES

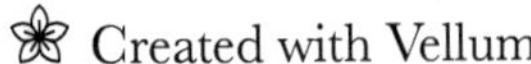
Created with Vellum

NOTE FROM THE AUTHOR

Thank you so much for picking up this book. Though this is the third book in the "Are you listening?" series, it is different from what I normally write. These books often take me longer because I feel they are so important that they have to be truly inspired.

This was not my original plan for the 3rd book. As book two ends with the rapture, my plan was to have Raven and the others dealing with the Tribulation in much more of a post-apocalypse way.

Then Covid-19 hit and my life, like yours I'm sure, was changed forever.

While on lockdown from my job and my gym, I began to research this virus a lot. I looked at both sides as I teach my students to do, and I traveled down some rabbit holes. One of those holes was a video of a woman talking about the Human Implantable quantum dot micro-needle vaccination delivery system supposedly patented by a famous philanthropist who will remain nameless here, and it made me wonder what if…

What if they could put this on Band-Aids? What if they could infect us without us even knowing? The original story was going to focus solely on Lily and the view of a high schooler, but as things in the world kept happening, I began to wonder if what we are seeing now is part of the end times.

I know there are a few views of the end times, and none of us really know for sure. I tend to believe the rapture will happen first because I have a hard time believing God would allow Christians to suffer through the tribulation, but there are others who believe the rapture will happen half way through and others who believe the rapture will happen at the end of the tribulation. There are still others who don't believe a rapture will happen at all.

Even though I wanted to write about the world today (and I don't believe the rapture has happened), I felt that this book should pick up where A Spark in Darkness left off, right after the rapture. One of my ARC readers said she had trouble with this part because like me she doesn't believe the rapture has happened yet. So, I'm asking you to imagine with me a little.

This book is mainly fiction, but I have included

elements that actually happened to me and are based on research I have done.

Some will not agree with the premise of the virus in this book that is close to Covid and that's okay. I do understand that while I have not been affected severely by it, others have. However, I also know there have been exaggerations and false claims surrounding it.

Some of you will not agree with my feelings that this vaccine may not be safe, and that's okay too. I pray daily for the safety of everyone affected by Covid and those who feel the vaccine is in their best interest, including many of my own family members. I pray that some of the things I'm reading about it will turn out to be false.

As I said before, this book is fiction laced with truth, but like many speculative authors before me, I hope that I'm wrong, and that my fiction does not prove reality. However, I have included as many links in the back as I can to what I did research. Regardless of what you decide, I urge you to do your own digging, and if you can't access some of my sites, then try using DuckDuckGo as your browser. Google censors a lot.

I have seen enough in this last year to tell me that we can no longer trust the media - either side. At least, not completely. In some cases, we cannot even trust what we see and hear, but we can always trust the still small voice inside of us that is the Holy Spirit. Use that as you search for the truth, and I have no doubt you will not be misled.

And if, after reading this, you feel the need for a lighter, feel good story to lift you up, you can sign up for my newsletter and get the first book in my Sweet Billionaires series for free.

Sign up for Lorana Hoopes's newsletter and get her book, The Billionaire's Impromptu Bet, as a welcome gift. Get Started Now!

I

JUST AFTER THE RAPTURE

"Raven, where are you going?" Jason stood a few feet from the entrance to the gym, a purple bruise already forming on the side of his face. He was an amazing trainer and fast as lightning, but he'd obviously been hit by something when the car crashed through the window. "Brian's called an ambulance and the police. He wants everyone to stay put until this gets sorted out."

Raven shook her head. "I have to get to Kat's house. She left me something that explains all this. Something I'm going to need." She turned back to assess her options. The main entrance to the gym parking lot was no good. People wandering around aimlessly blocked it, and an accident filled all four lanes of College Street less than a block from the exit. Perhaps the back entrance would be passable. That street saw less traffic, so she might get lucky enough to be able to weave through whatever cars might be there.

"Need? For what?" Exasperation threaded Jason's normally even tone. "Right now we need to find the kids and Kat. Where is Kat anyway?" His eyes wandered to Kat's blue Mini Cooper still parked in the space nearest the side door.

Raven bit the inside of her lip. What was going to happen to Kat's car? Or the rest of her stuff? Did she have family who would come looking for her? People that Raven should notify? How would she even know?

She turned back to Jason, intensity in her eyes. "Kat is gone, Jason. The kids are gone. We could search forever, but we'll never find them."

"Gone? Gone where?"

"Come with me. I'll show you and hopefully it will all make sense." Raven motioned for him to follow her even though she actually had no idea what would be waiting for her at Kat's place. Nor did she know if he would believe her. She certainly hadn't been easy to convince, and one thing she'd always liked about Jason was that he didn't buy into crazy theories. This was definitely the craziest theory she'd ever entertained, but suddenly she didn't want to do it alone. She didn't want to go into Kat's house, find nothing, and realize the last week had been some bad hallucination, but even more than that, she didn't want to find something that proved Kat was right and not have someone there with her.

Was this why she'd been left behind? Because she still doubted? She'd been about to tell Kat she believed before the disappearances, but did she really?

Jason's gaze flicked back to the gym door, and Kat shook her head. "You can stay if you want, but no answers reside in there. I can give you answers if you come with me."

His curiosity won out as she figured it would, and he followed her to her Jeep. After they were both buckled in, she fired up the engine and the radio blasted forth the emergency broadcast warning.

"This is an emergency alert. People are being encouraged to stay inside their houses. At least five planes have fallen from the sky over Washington state leaving fires and catastrophes in their wake."

"Wait, planes are falling from the sky?" Jason turned his attention to the sky out the window. "How is that even possible? Was this a terrorist attack?"

Raven sighed as she turned the key. "No, this affected the world, and those missing people aren't coming back."

"How do you know?"

Jason said the words slowly, cautiously, and his face wore the one expression she had hoped to never see on it. The one that said he thought she was nuts and might even regret getting in the car with her.

Raven avoided Jason's question as she looked behind her before throwing the Jeep in reverse and backing out. Could she tell him the truth? Did she truly believe? Once she uttered these words, their relationship would change forever. Was she really ready to do that?

Believe! The word floated through her mind like a whisper and carried the hint of Kat's voice. Raven stepped on the brakes, took a deep breath, and turned to Jason. "I know because Kat told me just like she told you. These people are gone because they were raptured, and now I'm pretty sure I have a job to do."

His eyes searched hers as if looking for the joke, the catch, but she didn't have time for him to catch on. She threw the Jeep into drive and gunned it, causing Jason to grip the dashboard with white knuckles.

For a moment he said nothing, and they traversed the street in silence. Then, finally, he uttered three words. "Job? What job?"

But Raven didn't answer. She didn't know the answer. She only had the few pieces that Kat had been able to tell her. The truth was she didn't really know what the future held.

She felt she was supposed to be some sort of guide and she knew that a ton of people had disappeared and that more bad events were coming, but that was the extent of her facts.

"I don't know. I'm hoping I'll figure it out when we get there."

They continued the rest of the way in silence which Raven was thankful for as she needed to focus on navigating the obstacles in the road. Even though this way was less heavily trafficked, there were still accidents and dazed people wandering the streets. Finally, Raven pulled up to Kat's house.

"Moment of truth," Raven said as she put the jeep in park and turned off the engine.

"What is it you think Kat left you?" Jason asked as they stepped on her front stoop.

Raven bent down and retrieved the key from under the welcome mat, just where Kat had said it would be. "I'm not sure exactly. She just said she left something for me. Something that would help explain all of this and what's coming." Even in Kat's normally quiet neighborhood, the sound of sirens and confusion carried on the breeze.

She inserted the key into the lock and pushed open the door. It felt weird stepping into Kat's living room. It would have been weird even if Kat were still here as the two hadn't been friends, but there was something even eerier knowing that Kat wouldn't be coming back here.

Her touch was still palpable in the room; Raven could see it in the arrangement of the furniture and the placement of the pictures. She could feel it in the carefree way the shoes were placed by the front door and the way a recently-worn sweater draped across the back of a chair. A sweater that would never be worn again.

Raven wandered the room, hoping whatever Kat had left for her would be obvious. Though she was not above snooping through drawers, the thought felt a little like disturbing a dead body.

"Well, she certainly was neat," Jason said as he too walked through the room. "Hey, Raven?"

"Yeah?" She scanned the coffee table for any sort of clue, but there were only a few magazines.

"You might want to come here for a second."

Raven put the magazines back in place and crossed to the kitchen where Jason stood staring down at the table. An unlit but half burned candle sat in the middle surrounded by a plastic wreath, but she was pretty sure it was the small black book and journal that had garnered his attention. Sticking out from the journal was a white envelope with her name across the side.

With trembling fingers, she pulled the envelope the rest of the way out of the journal and opened it. A single sheet of white paper was folded inside. She pulled it out and read the pretty cursive.

Dear Raven,

If you are reading this, then it means I'm gone. Hopefully, it was due to the rapture and not some tragic accident. I wish I'd had more time to research and talk to people who really studied this, so I could pass on more information for you, but what I can tell you is that the next few years will not be easy. The Bible isn't exactly clear on what will come, but it is clear that it will not be an easy time. Famine, earthquakes, and lawlessness are mentioned, but in this day and age, the tribulations could be anything. You'll need to keep a vigilant eye, especially for anything that creates dissension or instills fear in people.

Also, at some point, a figure will emerge who will claim to be able to unite the world in harmony. I assume this figure will be a man, but again, don't discount anything. Do your homework on anyone who claims to be able to do something that seems too good to be true, and listen for anything that seems to go against God's word. I know you haven't been a believer in your past and you may not have your own, so I'm entrusting my Bible and my journal to you. I've marked passages I thought were important as well as written my thoughts in the journal.

One more thing. In Revelation, there is talk of a "mark of the beast." Though no one knows exactly what this will be, most assume it will be some numbers or symbol that people take. Many will line up to take it willingly and those who do not will be killed. The mark will probably become a requirement to do certain things though that is just speculation that I've read. My point is that you need to be aware of it. Anything the government wants you to take, you should research. These will be trying times, and I wish I could have left you with more guidance. Search for others like yourself - those who realized too late or knew but chose a different path. Unite with them and learn all you can. Try to rebuild the churches as they will be needed now more than ever and help those who will be grieving.

Know that I will be praying for you and counting down the hours until I can see you again.

Kat

Raven lowered the letter and looked at Jason. "I think this is what I was looking for." She tucked the letter back in the envelope and picked up the Bible and journal.

"Don't tell me you actually believe all that," Jason said. Raven could tell that he was having the same internal battle she was - only she was confident she was closer to fully believing than he was.

"Do you have a better explanation?" she asked, throwing the ball into his court. She'd tried to come up with anything that could explain Micah and the dark shapes she'd seen the last few days, but all roads had led back to Kat.

"I just…" his brow furrowed, and he sighed, "No, at the moment I do not, but I will come up with one."

Raven chuckled wryly. "Yeah, that's what I thought too. Come on, we should get back to the gym and help Brian with the clean-up. It looks like we'll have a lot of that in our future."

Dr. Candace Markham grabbed the railing of the hospital bed as she felt the ground shake beneath her. "What was that?" she asked the nurse on duty once it stilled.

The nurse, a woman in her late twenties or early thirties by the name of Julie, looked up at Candace with wide eyes full of fear. "I have no idea. Earthquake?"

"I don't think so," Candace said. "Too short." She turned her attention to their patient, a man who'd been in a hit and run, but he seemed stable for the moment. "Page Dr. Edwards in surgery and tell him we're bringing one up." The scan had shown the patient had internal bleeding and though he was stable at the moment, Candace knew that wouldn't last long.

Julie nodded and crossed to the phone on the wall. She lifted the receiver, punched in a few buttons, and then asked for Dr. Edwards. Then her face fell. "Okay, is there anyone in surgery free?"

A knot of apprehension twisted in Candace's stomach. She couldn't hear the conversation, but it was clear from Julie's face that something was going on. Something that had to do with that shaking?

"What's the matter?" Candace asked when Julie returned to her side.

Julie blinked a few times as if in shock before finally managing to squeak a few words out. "They say Dr. Edwards disappeared."

"Disappeared? Well, did they bother paging him? He's probably taking a break somewhere."

"No." Julie shook her head. "The nurse said she saw him disappear."

"What?" Candace rolled her eyes; she didn't have time for this nonsense, but before she could say anything else, her pager went off. She glanced down at it. Emergency on the roof? Had a helicopter crashed? She supposed that could explain the previous shaking. It vibrated again. *Multiple crashes reported citywide. All hospitals to be on standby alert for patient overloads.*

"What is it?" Julie asked, clearly sensing something was wrong from the expression on Candace's face.

"Multiple crashes citywide. They say to brace for patient overload. What exactly is going on here? Look, get him up to surgery with whoever they can find and then get back here. It sounds like we'll need all hands on deck."

Julie nodded and Candace helped her get the bed wheeled into the hallway, but as the elevator door opened and Julie stepped inside, chaos erupted in the ER.

The sound of ceramic shattering sent Gabe Cross jumping to his feet. "Melinda, are you okay?"

His wife had been grabbing them both a mug of after-noon coffee - a rare treat around his house. Normally, he would be at work right now, and she would be wrangling the kids, but he'd finished work early, and she'd taken the kids to her mother's house, so it was just the two of them. They'd decided to have a cup of coffee and watch a movie before her mother brought the children home.

"Melinda?" He stepped into the kitchen and froze. Shattered pieces of mugs lay in a pool of brown liquid. At the edge of the liquid lay the jeans and sweater that Melinda had been wearing. Though he knew it was irrational, Gabe tore through the house calling her name, but she was nowhere to be found. That could only mean... The kids! The thought pierced him like a knife and he placed a hand against the wall as a vise squeezed his lungs. Would they be gone too?

When he could catch a breath, he pulled his phone from his pocket and dialed Melinda's mother's number, but all it did was ring. No, this could not be happening. Not now! Not yet!

Grabbing his keys, he hurried to the car. He had to find the kids. They couldn't be gone. Not all of them.

Lily dialed Katie as the sound of sirens grew louder around her. Normally she didn't mind being home alone after school. It gave her time to get a snack and unwind before her parents came home and peppered her with questions about how her day was, but right now, she didn't want to be alone.

"Lily, are you okay?" Katie was Lily's best friend, and she'd never heard the kind of fear she heard in her voice now.

"I think so, but the sirens are so loud. What's going on?"

"I don't know, but my neighbor is screaming that someone took her son. She's starting to freak me out. Are your parents home?"

"No, are yours?"

"No."

Lily took a deep breath and tried to remain calm. Even though Katie was as scared as she was, just having her on the phone helped. "It's okay. It will be okay." She moved to the window to glance outside, but not much seemed out of the ordinary there. Of course, she lived on a quiet residential street. Whatever had happened must have happened closer to the business side of town.

But what? An explosion? No, she would have heard that. A robbery? Possibly, but there were so many sirens and that didn't explain Katie's neighbors' kids.

Lily let the curtain fall back over the window and walked into the living room, her eyes searching for the remote. She clicked it on and stared at the images invading her television. Her breath escaped in a soft whoosh along with the strangled words, "Oh my gosh."

Pastor Benjamin Westley felt it. He didn't know what it was at first - a cold sensation, the kind that he imagined he would feel if a ghost ever passed through him, but then an immediate weight descended upon his shoulders. And he knew. He knew that Jesus had come and he'd been left behind.

Dropping his head to his hands, he began to sob. "I'm so sorry, Lord. Please forgive me but use me now. Let me be like Samson. Use me to save as many as possible. Please Lord."

2
THE FOLLOWING SUNDAY

Pastor Benjamin Westley wasn't sure if anyone would come to church, but there hadn't been a Sunday he hadn't opened the doors, and he wasn't about to start now. He had already fielded a few calls from parishioners who had been left behind, but he wasn't sure if they would show up. Most of them didn't understand what had happened - why they'd been left behind - and he was afraid the few who did wouldn't want to come hear what he had to say. After all, he'd been left behind too.

However, he knew he wasn't alone. When the disappearances hit and he realized what had happened, he'd cried and apologized to God. Then, he'd begun calling his friends who were also in the ministry. Most didn't answer, and he assumed they were gone, but a few had. They also had realized what had happened and lamented with him, feigning disbelief that they were still here. Ben knew why though.

What he'd realized after hanging up with the others was that they had all been avoiding preaching The Word. The world was changing rapidly, and tolerance was the message of the masses. That meant there were suddenly a lot of topics that were off limits for fear of offending someone, and God help him, instead of standing firm in the word of God, he'd succumbed.

No more. If anyone returned to church, Ben would be teaching from the Bible, and he didn't care who he offended.

The building was cold and dark as he opened the door. How sad it felt without the people. Would any of them return? Would this place ever fill up again? He flicked the lights on and realized he didn't know how to make everything in this place work. Someone else usually handled the sound system and the singing and the greeting. A sigh bubbled up within him; he had no idea if any of those people were left, and he rather hoped they weren't. Thankfully, he knew where the thermostat was, so he headed there first and flicked it on to get the place warmed up.

"Pastor Ben? Are you here?"

Ben recognized that voice as he rounded the corner. Nathan, one of the sound guys. Though saddened that

Nathan had been left behind, he was thankful for the company.

"Nathan, how are you, my friend?" Ben asked as he greeted the man and placed a hand on his shoulder.

Nathan was a big guy, nearly six feet and close to three hundred pounds, but the man's face crumbled at Ben's touch.

"They're gone, Pastor Ben. Heidi, the kids, my parents. Everyone is gone."

Ben led the man to the chairs inside the sanctuary. "I know, Nathan. It's hard, but we will see them again."

"Why, Pastor? Why weren't we taken too?"

Ben knew he would be asked this question a lot in the future, however much of the future he had. It would never get easier, but this first time would have to be the hardest. "Well, Nathan, the Bible says that some will call him Lord but not really believe. As for me, I know that I lost my faith when Beth died last year." Cancer had taken her, but Ben had blamed God. "I stopped preaching the words God wanted me to preach and turned to what the world wanted. I lost my way." Ben softened his tone and leaned toward Nathan. "Do you think there's something that caused you to lose your way?"

Nathan looked down at the floor and shook his head slowly. "This weight. I guess more of my identity was tied up in my job than I thought, and when I lost it, I slowly lost myself. I couldn't seem to stop eating, and the more I gained, the more I hated myself, the more I thought I wasn't worthy."

"That was Satan in your ear," Ben said. "God always thought you were worthy, and he doesn't care what you look like on the outside though he does appreciate when we keep our bodies healthy. They are His temple after all."

Nathan nodded and then slowly lifted his head. "What do we do now, Pastor Ben?"

"Now, we believe. Completely. We follow God's law and we tell everyone we can what happened. Unfortunately, the Bible says it won't be easy until we get to Heaven, but we will get there, Nathan."

Nathan took a few steadying breaths. "Okay." The word came out more as a sigh, but it was a start. He placed his hands on his knees. "Should I get the sound system fired up?"

"I think we can wait on that a bit, Nathan," Ben said. "It might be just the two of us today."

"Hello? Is there anyone here?"

"Or not," Nathan said with a slight smile.

Ben didn't recognize the woman's voice, but he stood and walked out to the foyer to greet whoever it might be. He could feel Nathan behind him, a large and protective presence, though he wasn't sure he would need it. The woman was young with dark hair and an edgy air. He didn't know all the parishioners in the church as well as he would have liked, but he was certain he'd never seen her before.

"Hello, I'm Pastor Ben. How can I help you?"

Her brow lifted as she folded her arms across her chest. "A pastor. Well, I didn't expect to actually find one of you left behind. I figured I'd have to settle for an intern or something."

"I'm sorry?"

"No, I'm sorry," she said, dropping her arms. "I'm forgetting my manners." She took a few steps toward him and held out her hand. "My name is Raven Rader, and I think I was meant to find you."

Ben blinked at her. "Well, I'm certainly glad that you found me, but why do you think you were meant to find me?"

"Can we sit down? My story is kind of long."

"Sure. This is Nathan by the way. He handles our sound system although I doubt we'll need it today." Pastor Ben led the way to the sanctuary. He and Nathan turned a few chairs around so that the group faced each other. "The floor is yours," Ben said, leaning back in the chair.

Raven chewed on her lip before taking a deep breath and beginning. "A few weeks ago, I met this girl named Kat who said she saw angels. She told me that I was going to play a role in what came next. I didn't believe her, but then I started seeing dark shapes, shapes I now believe were demons, though I haven't seen them since the disappearances.

"Before Kat was taken, she told me she left something for me at her house. I went with a friend of mine and found this letter in a journal along with her Bible. I've never been a believer, and I am not familiar with the Bible, so she told me to find others who are. I'm hoping that's where you come in."

Ben leaned forward, intrigued by the woman's story. "I can certainly help you understand the Bible. I may have lost my way, but I understand the words."

"Good, because somehow, I'm supposed to tell those who are left what's about to come, and I have no idea how to do that."

"What if you did it virtually?" Nathan asked. He had been silent up to this point, and he now looked sheepish as if unsure he should have spoken.

"What do you mean? Like online?" Raven asked.

He shrugged. "Yeah, I watch a lot of YouTube and those people have thousands who follow them. What if you made videos like they did? We could even record your sermons, Pastor Ben, and send them out. That would reach way more people than we could do by ourselves."

Pastor Ben looked to the woman who appeared deep in thought. Her dark hair covered her face, so he couldn't see her expression, but when she lifted her head, she was smiling.

"Nathan, I think that's a great idea."

Candace Markham stared at the Bible she hadn't read in ages. Her fingers trembled as she let them glide across the dark leather cover. She'd known or at least she'd assumed as soon as the patients began flooding in that day. Most had been involved in automobile accidents when either the person they'd been driving with had disappeared or a car with no driver had hit them. A few people had been hit while walking, and one person had been injured from flying debris when a plane crashed near him. Regardless of the injury, all the stories had been the same. Someone had disappeared.

Candace remembered the pain that had gripped her heart as she treated one patient after another. She'd had no time to call her husband, but she'd known it wouldn't have mattered. He would be gone. She'd been attending church with him as long as they'd been married, but that's all she had been doing - attending. At the end of the sermons on the Sundays she could attend, she could rarely recall the message because she'd been too busy thinking about her job to actually listen to the words.

Phil had tried to talk to her in those rare moments they'd had together, but she'd brushed him off. She liked the idea of God - someone who was there when you needed Him, but she hadn't actually wanted to change her lifestyle, and she'd heard too many people who'd spoken about giving up things they loved to follow God's plan. She'd always thought there would be time for God's plan, when she was done with her own. Turned out, she'd been wrong.

When she'd finally gotten home the day after the disasters, Phil had been gone and the house had been empty, just as she'd known it would be. She'd expected to feel something - sadness, anger, shock, something, but all she'd felt was nothing. A deep, empty void of nothing. So, she'd showered and crawled into bed, pulling his pillow toward her. It had been strange. They rarely shared their bed anymore due to her demanding schedule, but at that moment, all she'd wanted was something to remind her of him.

She'd stayed in bed all of Tuesday and returned to work on Wednesday where it had been just as hectic as Monday evening. Several of their staff had gone missing and more causalities had come in while she'd been out.

"The government is now claiming the disappearances are a terrorist attack from Russia though they have yet to supply any proof of how Russia might have pulled this off."

Candace shook her head and smirked at the newscaster on the television. She'd turned it on for noise in hopes it would lessen the lonely feeling pervading her house, but she hadn't really been listening until now. However, at the word that had seemed to own the previous year, she focused her attention on the newscaster.

Russia! Though she had no doubt that Russia played a part in some of the nefarious activity the government reported on, how anyone could say the country was at fault here with a straight face was beyond her. People had disappeared from all over the world, including Russia, but then again, these newscasters probably had no idea about the rapture or had probably hardened their hearts like she had. She wondered how many others like her might be out there - people who had known but hadn't really believed. Could she find more like herself? She could try, but it could wait until after she caught up on some reading.

With a sigh, Candace flipped open the Bible and began reading.

Gabe shook his head at the television as the anchor spoke of the newest theory that aliens were involved in the mass disappearances six days previously. Just a few minutes ago, the media had claimed the disappearances were Russia's fault though they'd never been able to explain how Russia vaporized people or why certain people had disappeared while others had not. Add to that the fact that Russia suffered their own disappearances and Gabe wasn't surprised they'd had to cancel that theory, but he was slightly surprised they'd gone with aliens. It wasn't that Gabe didn't believe in aliens - he had heard enough stories to at least be open to the possibilities of aliens, but why take so many of the population? What would that accomplish?

As the news anchor flashed up pictures of the recently released information for Area 51 as if that explained everything, Gabe clicked the channel changer. He didn't believe it was aliens any more than he had believed it was Russia, and neither of them got his family back or filled the void in his heart.

Melinda and the kids had been gone for six days. Six long days. No matter where they were, could they even still be alive? Melinda's mother had been gone as well when he'd finally reached her house which gave him hope that at least the kids weren't alone, but where were they? And more importantly, how did he get them back?

He paused as the image of a man with scraggly hair and wild eyes filled the screen. "I'm telling you it was the rapture," he said to whomever was interviewing him. "God got tired of us turning our backs on him, and He took them home."

"You sound like a believer," the off-camera voice said.

The man nodded. "I am."

"Yet, you're claiming God took the believers-"

Another nod. "He did."

"Then why are you still here?"

As if realizing he'd walked into a trap, the man opened and closed his mouth a few times before his shoulders dropped. The craze went out of his eyes, replaced with a deep sadness. "I guess I only thought I was a believer."

The camera cut to the interviewer who shook his head. "And there you have it folks, the rapture could be another theory for the disappearances, but you'd have to be a little crazy to believe it."

The camera panned back to the man, but Gabe no longer saw crazy. He saw himself in the man's dejected shoulders and downcast eyes. The man had obviously lost people close to him. Could he be right? Could it have been the rapture? Gabe remembered Melinda talking about it, pleading with him to believe so he wouldn't be left behind, but he'd thought it, like a lot of the things in the Bible, was something taken out of context. There were so many rules that couldn't really be requirements in the culture of today which had led him to believe that the Bible, while it may have been important to the people of the time, held no relevance in today's society. But had he been wrong? Had he been left behind?

3

TWO MONTHS LATER

"Are you sure now is the time, sir? The economy is just starting to recover after the rapture. This could throw it into chaos again." Samael bowed his head to avoid looking Daman directly in the eyes. It was not in his nature to question his lord, but the timing did not seem appropriate to him.

"Chaos is exactly what we need, Samael." Daman rose from his throne and paced the dark room. "After the rapture, the churches were empty, the people blamed each other. We were this close to an all-out war." He held his long, pale fingers less than an inch apart. "But now they are beginning to fill again," he said with disdain. "People - these hapless creatures God created - are searching for meaning again. We must shut that down. Turn them back to things of the flesh. If we can strike fear into them again, they will be desperate for a savior."

"A savior like you, sir?" Samael lifted his face slightly now that it seemed Daman was not angry.

A sinister smile pulled at Daman's lips. "Indeed. A savior like me. Once we infect the world with this virus, we can sow dissent, fear, hate. Get the people in power to spread the fear and keep the people locked inside. Then, I can emerge with a cure that will end the misery." He spread his arms wide. "They will trip over themselves in the race to save themselves, to return to normal. They will clamor to appoint me ruler over all. By the time we are done with them, few will pause long enough to consult scriptures that have mostly been forgotten anyway."

Samael swallowed audibly. "But what of those who do, sir? What will we do about them? If the virus does not take them?"

Daman's dark eyes twinkled as he steepled his hands together. "Don't you worry. I have plans for any who may resist our cause. They will be examples, useful if they do emerge. Now, do we have a patient?"

Samael nodded. "We do." He crossed to a door that lay nearly hidden in the room. Only a slight line indicated that the wall was disturbed. With a deft touch, he opened the door and rolled the man out. The man, having been tied to the chair and locked in the room for hours, had little fight left in him and said not a word, as if he thought what awaited him outside would be better than the dark solitude of the room. Samael almost felt sorry for him. Almost.

After placing the man and the chair in front of Daman, Samael returned to the hidden room and grabbed the vial from the fridge. He held it up to the light, swishing it slightly as the men had told him to do. Then he grabbed a syringe as well before returning.

"How long will it take?" Daman asked as he watched Samael fill the vial.

"The scientists were unsure of a specific timeline, but they believe between twelve and twenty-four hours for the virus to take hold. However, he will be contagious long before he begins showing symptoms which will facilitate the spread of the disease."

Daman rubbed his hands together. "That will be perfect. And he won't remember this?"

Samael shook his head. "No, the scientists assured me that he will have no memory of today at all."

"Wonderful. Proceed."

Samael stuck the syringe into the vial and then injected the liquid into the man's arm. A slight twitch and a grimace was all the man could muster, but that was understandable considering the ordeal he had been through. "Don't worry. For you at least, this will all be over soon."

When the syringe was empty, Samael summoned an

attendant to return the man to his work. The attendant would then be killed, but it was a small price to pay to make sure nothing could be traced back to either himself or, more importantly, Daman.

When the man and the attendant were gone, Daman returned to his throne. A look of pure malicious delight twisted his features. "And now we wait. Let the fun begin."

Candace took a deep breath to calm her nerves as she approached the building. After poring through her Bible for the last several weeks, she'd realized three things. First, there was still a lot of it that she didn't understand, and she needed to talk to someone who could help her understand it. Second, she had to discover the truth. Was the rapture really the cause for Phil's disappearance? And if it was, that led to question number three. What was coming next? She remembered Phil talking about the book of Revelation and what it said about end times, but she hadn't been listening at the time. Not *really* listening anyway. Like with most things, she'd nodded and acted as if she understood while her mind had been a million miles away.

But she was listening now, and that had led her to her computer and to a website named Truth Seekers. At first, she'd just poked around the site, reading the belief statement and watching the videos that were uploaded each Sunday - after all, she couldn't be caught talking about the rapture in her line of work. It was not considered science, and the people who had dared to speak out about the rapture had been decimated on social media as crazies, loons. Most would probably never get a job again. However, even knowing that, the feeling that Candace needed to see this place in person, connect with these people, would not leave her and seemed to grow heavier by the day. So, here she was.

The parking lot wasn't even half full, and Candace wondered briefly if it had been before the disappearances. By the size of the building, she thought it must have.

A large man stood at the door - the kind of man who looked more like he belonged at the door of a nightclub as a bouncer than at the entrance of a church as a greeter - but the smile he flashed as Candace approached softened his image.

"Welcome to Mountain Home, I'm Nathan." He held out a single sheet of paper to her.

Candace took the paper and scanned it. It appeared to be a short order of worship - a few songs, prayer, message - and some links for connections. "Thank you, I'm Candace, but I haven't been in a church in a long time."

Nathan's smile widened, and he nodded sagely. "Don't worry. We're all pretty new to The Word here."

Candace wasn't quite sure what he meant by that, but

she returned his smile and entered the building. The immediate vicinity was obviously a foyer as she could see into the sanctuary a few feet ahead of her and the paths to either side appeared to be hallways to other rooms.

"Hi, you look new," a woman to her right said.

Candace turned to see a young, edgy woman with dark hair smiling at her. "Uh, yeah, first time, but I've been following the website for a few weeks."

The woman's eyes lit up. "I'm so glad. I'm Raven and I'm in charge of the website, and it's always nice to hear that it's actually doing what it was created to do."

"And what was it created to do?" Candace asked.

"Unite those who seek the truth. The world is going to get crazier, but we're trying to help as many people as we can."

"What do you mean crazier?" Candace asked. She should be unnerved or at least skeptical of this woman and this conversation but all Candace felt was peace.

Raven cocked her head as if studying Candace. "I'm guessing you're here because you lost someone in the disappearances."

"Didn't we all?" Candace asked with a slight chuff. She certainly didn't know anyone who had been spared. Not everyone had lost a spouse or a close family member as she had, but everyone seemed to know someone who was now missing.

"We did. The difference is that we know what really

happened, and if you're here, my guess is you suspect the truth as well."

"The rapture?" Candace asked even though the words felt taboo on her lips.

Raven issued a soft smile and nodded. "And if you're familiar with the rapture, then surely you know what comes next." She lifted her brows as if asking that silent question.

Candace thought back over what she'd been reading. She didn't understand most of it, which was why she was here, but she knew enough to know what came next. "The tribulation."

"That's right," Raven said. "We don't know exactly what it will look like or how it will come, but we meet every Sunday to discuss ideas and new ways to reach people like yourself. There is a war coming, and we are trying to be prepared."

A war? Candace thought. *How could they possibly face a war? And how could it be harder than what they'd gone through the last few months?* Candace wondered if there was more to her showing up here than mild curiosity, but she'd come this far, she might as well hear them out.

4

ONE MONTH LATER

"Lily, you better get down here if you want breakfast while it's warm." Her mother's voice carried up the stairs and it held the note of annoyance Lily was used to hearing from her mother when she was working on her last nerve.

With a sigh, Lily turned off the curling iron and set it on the counter. Her hair wasn't being agreeable this morning, but it wasn't awful either. She tossed her head down and then up, tousled the blonde locks with her fingers, and decided it would have to do. Flicking off the bathroom light, she grabbed a jacket and headed downstairs. March was fickle in Washington state. Some days it was warm, others cool, but one thing she could count on was that it would start off cool enough to need a jacket.

The aroma of pancakes, syrup, and bacon met Lily's

nose before she entered the kitchen, and she sighed. None of that was on her current eating plan. It wasn't that she was overweight, but she definitely was curvier than most of her peers. When she got older, she figured she would enjoy that, but right now, she was sixteen and in high school. Anything over the perfectly accepted limit of tiny was too much, so she decided to skip the pancakes and grab a piece of fruit from the fridge and a cup of coffee instead.

"You should not be drinking coffee so young," her mother said with a shake of her head. "I didn't start drinking coffee until I was well into my twenties."

"I know, Mom. You tell me that every day." Lily turned away from her and rolled her eyes as she grabbed the creamer and added a dose. Rolling her eyes at her mother was a sure-fire way to get grounded, and she could not be grounded anytime soon. The Spring Fling dance at her high school was approaching, and she had been looking forward to it for weeks. Her dress was picked, her hair appointment was set, and her date was a gorgeous boy by the name of Bryce Hawkins.

"Can't you at least have some toast or an egg with that fruit?" Her mother's face wrinkled in concern, sending tiny lines stretching out from the corner of her mouth and eyes. "I can't see how one piece of fruit will fill you up until lunch. You need some protein."

What her mother didn't know was that one piece of

fruit didn't fill Lily up until lunch, but her best friend Katie always had snacks and because she loved Lily so much, she always shared. That generally held her over until lunch, and on days when it didn't, she would break down and purchase a muffin from the kitchen during morning break time. Yes, the calories were unfathomable, but she always made sure to run an extra mile as well as attend the gym on those days to balance it out. "I'll be fine, Mom."

She set her mug and orange down on the counter and opened the pantry. "Look, I'll even take a protein bar if it'll make you feel better." Lily held the bar up for her mother's inspection and sighed with relief when her mother threw her hands up and shook her head. She had won the battle. For now.

Before she had a chance to enjoy her meager breakfast, the alarm on her phone began chiming, reminding her it was time to get going. After shoving the bar in her pocket - she'd have to remember to put it in her backpack in the car or she'd have a melted mess when she got around to eating it - she took one last swig of her coffee and gave her mother a quick peck on the cheek. "Be back at five," she hollered as she made her way out the front door.

Lily slid into the seat of her slightly used Ford Taurus. It was not the car she had wanted for her birthday, but it was better than nothing. She fished the protein bar out of her pocket and tossed it and her bag on the passenger seat.

Then she turned up the music and backed out of the driveway. She didn't live far from the school, but the drive jamming out to her favorite music was the perfect way to start the day. If she had to attend school, she might as well do it right.

Her best friend Katie was waiting for her as she pulled into the parking lot. She generally made it to school before Lily did. In fact, there had been times when Lily wondered if she slept at the building some nights. Katie loved school, and not the walking-the-halls-and-seeing-friends side of school. No, she was the nose-in-the-book-studying-and-learning type of student, so she generally met Lily before she made it to her locker each morning. However, waiting at her parking spot was new.

"Did you hear?" she asked, handing Lily a cup of coffee as she climbed out of the car. Katie was a Starbucks snob and she ordered one nearly every morning, but Lily didn't mind since coffee was partly how she got her fuel anyway.

She took a sip of the proffered cup, enjoying the warmth that spread down her throat. Though no longer winter, the cold seemed to hang around a lot longer in the state of Washington, and it was still chilly this morning. "Hear what?" Lily didn't watch the news and Katie knew that. If it didn't involve Lily directly, it didn't usually end up on her radar.

"There's an outbreak in China of some virus."

"Seriously?" Lily's ears perked up. Though current events were not her forte, a pandemic was her one morbid curiosity. Ever since the day she'd read The Stand by Stephen King, she'd been fascinated by pandemics. It wasn't that she wanted one to happen, it was more like she wondered how one could happen, how it would affect the world, and what it would be like to live through one.

"Yeah, seriously." She flipped her long brown hair over one shoulder as she fell into step beside Lily. "I can't believe you don't watch the news. I bet Mr. Higgins makes us study it."

Mr. Higgins was their science teacher, but he must have taught at a college once because he was the hardest teacher in the school. His papers were the bane of Lily's - and every other non-studious student's - existence. "Ugh, I hope he doesn't make us do a paper on it." Papers were the quickest way to steal her interest in any subject.

"He probably will. Plus, I bet he makes us research the disease and track the possibility of it reaching over here. Maybe he'll even let us dig more into viruses and how they work." Her eyes lit up as she rambled off the options. She was such a nerd that Lily sometimes wondered how they stayed friends, but it was probably because they'd known each other since birth.

Their mothers had met at some prenatal yoga class and become fast friends. As they lived near each other, their friendship had continued even after the girls were born with playdates and get-togethers. Katie and Lily had been destined to be friends no matter what they did. Thankfully, they seemed to balance each other well. Katie was more studious and helped keep Lily academically focused, but she also had a tendency to believe crazy theories, and Lily kept her more grounded in reality.

"Yeah, well, let's not give him any ideas. I don't mind talking about it, but I don't want to research it for the next month. The Spring Fling is coming up, and I have much more important ways to spend my time." *Like slow dancing in Bryce's arms,* she thought to herself, picturing the moment in her mind.

Bryce was a senior and one Lily had set her sights on since Freshman year. She hadn't thought he would ever notice her, but somehow, miraculously, this year he had. She didn't know if it was the fact that she finally had a class with him or the fact that she'd ditched her oversized tunics and leggings for skinny jeans and tighter shirts. Whatever the reason, she'd caught his eye, and two weeks ago, he'd asked her to the Spring Fling.

The Spring Fling was as close to a prom as their small school got. They didn't have the money or the student numbers to hold a large prom, but the school would generally rent out a nice banquet hall and cater dinner. Students would dress up in formal attire and dance the night away. Lily looked forward to it every year, but this year was guaranteed to top them all.

Science was her first class of the day, and the room was already abuzz with conversation. Hannah and Gretchen both had their phones out and were taking turns flashing their screens at each other as they found some story they wanted to share. Christian and Adam sat side by side peering into a laptop screen. Evidently, Lily was one of the few who hadn't watched the news. Only Isaiah seemed unphased by the information. As usual, he was digging in his backpack like he did every morning. Lily and Katie took their seats and waited for the bell to ring.

"All right," Mr. Higgins said as soon as the bell stopped. "I'm sure you've all heard about the virus by now." An older man with a receding hairline and a salt and pepper goatee, Mr. Higgins reminded Lily slightly of Mr. Rogers. At least until he began assigning essays.

Katie shot her a look with raised eyebrows as if to say "See? I told you so."

"So, let's discuss what we know about viruses in general and what we know about this one." A sinister gleam danced in his eyes as he clapped his hands together, and Lily stifled a sigh. There would be more than one paper around this virus.

As the discussion waged on around her, Lily found herself being drawn in. Though no one really knew how the virus had originated, what was known was that the first diagnosed patient was a technician at a lab in China. Evidently, he'd thought he just had a cold or a mild case of the flu. However, a week later, his lungs began to shut down and he was placed on a ventilator. While he was unconscious, four more people from his lab also became sick, and the number increased from there. It appeared that although patient zero had recovered, many others had not, and the death count was now nearing the hundreds in China and the surrounding areas.

The news media was referring to it as NCAV or a novel contagious airborne virus. The novel aspect evidently came from the fact that it had markers and qualities that had never been seen before.

"Mr. Higgins, is there any way this virus could come to us?" The question had been posed by Hannah, a quiet, studious girl, but Lily was pretty sure it was the question on all of the students' minds. She watched Mr. Higgins eagerly as he tried to formulate his answer.

After a large deep breath, he sighed and looked them all in the eyes as he said, "I'm not sure."

"What does this mean for us?" Candace asked as she glanced around the room. Doctors from nearly every department filled the room.

"We don't know yet," Dr. Aikens, the hospital chief, said. In his late sixties, he was a stern man with gray hair and a paunch belly. His muscular arms hinted that he had been in shape at one time though. "What we do know is that it is highly unlikely the virus won't make it here and we need to be prepared. We have some PPE, but not enough for what they're saying we will need. However, we have a request with the governor for more, and I've heard talk that the President is offering assistance."

He paused as if surveying the room. "I'm not going to lie. We are on the front lines, and we don't know much about what we're fighting. Remember the most important pieces. Wash your hands, get plenty of rest, and gear up. Every time." He paused to look each one of them in the eye. "Okay, I know that's a lot, but does anyone have any questions?"

Candace had a plethora of questions racing through her mind, but none that Dr. Aikens could answer. No, she needed to call Raven and Pastor Ben and get their take on this. As much as she didn't want to admit, she had a very bad feeling that this might be the beginning of the tribulation Raven had spoken of.

As soon as they were dismissed, Candace excused herself to an on-call room and dialed Raven's number. She didn't even bother with pleasantries when the other woman answered. "Is this it? Do you think this is the beginning?"

Raven sighed on the other end. "I'm assuming you mean the virus."

"Of course I mean the virus," Candace snapped. "I

just left a briefing where we were told to gear up and get ready for it. I just want your opinion. Do you think this is it?"

"I don't know, but it could be. I'll start looking, Candace, and we'll talk more on Sunday, but promise me one thing."

"What's that?" Candace asked although she was fairly certain she knew what Raven would ask.

"Be careful."

That seemed to be the theme of the day around her. "I will," Candace promised before hanging up the phone, but if the virus was the beginning of the tribulation, could she ever really be careful enough?

"What we know now is that the NCAV has appeared in countries outside of China. Cases have appeared in London, Italy, and Germany, but the President and his team continue to state there is no reason for worry here in the United States. Though he was originally vilified for the action, it appears the President closed the borders to travel from China last month and remains confident that action will keep the virus from breaching our borders."

Raven felt a claw-like sensation squeeze her heart, and her fingers began to play with the cross around her neck.

She'd told Candace she wasn't sure this was the beginning of the end, but the more coverage she watched of it, the more she became convinced that it would have a role to play.

She jumped to her feet. Kat's letter. She needed to read it again. Though she hadn't really understood what the letter meant at the time, she had taken it and the Bible and journal with her nearly everywhere she went and had studied it with every free moment. The Sunday after the rapture, she'd met Pastor Ben, who while having been left behind, at least seemed to have more knowledge of the word than she did. They'd begun studying Kat's words together, along with a few other people who had joined their small group.

That first day, it had just been herself, the pastor, and one other man by the name of Nathan, but they'd all agreed there had to be more like them out there. Raven had set up a website for the church advertising that the message of hope and truth was available every Sunday. Attendance had gradually increased to a group of about fifty now, and Pastor Ben said the other churches were also seeing a surge. Evidently, other people were beginning to search for the truth as well.

Raven scanned the letter again before grabbing her phone and dialing Pastor Ben.

"Are you watching the news?" she asked when he answered.

"I am."

"What can we do? Candace called me and told me they just had a safety briefing about it."

"I'm not sure. Right now, I guess we watch and wait, but I will admit that I'm scared for what this might mean for our church, especially since we have just started rebuilding. It appears they are already locking businesses down in China."

"They couldn't lock down things here, could they?" Raven couldn't imagine how that would work. The US was too big and the states were too different.

"I don't know, Raven. I just don't know. There is one thing we can do though. We can pray."

They ended the call and Raven stared at the news screen. They had already suffered so much with the loss of so many lives. Could they handle an unknown virus? And if not, what did that mean?

5

Candace had just finished her lunch when her pager went off. After glancing down at it, she threw her trash away and headed down to the ER.

"What's going on?" she asked the nurse on duty as she entered the area.

"We think we might have a case of NCAV." The woman's eyes were large and filled with fear. "They've put him in isolation and Julie is gathering up your gear."

"Right." Conflicting emotions flooded Candace. Common sense told her that she was prepared for this, that she had trained for this, but fear dominated that thought. Fear of the unknown. There was still so little they knew about this virus and what she had seen on the media made it out to be the worst killing machine in modern history.

No, she couldn't let fear control her. She knew how to keep herself safe or as safe as she could, and she'd found Jesus again. Even if it was her time, it just meant she would see Phil again that much sooner.

With a swift nod at the nurse, Candace continued to the isolation area. Sure enough, Julie was waiting outside, already geared up, with more gear for Candace on a table beside her. Most of her face was covered with a mask, but fear radiated around her like a palpable mist.

"What do we have?" Candace asked as she began the process of suiting up with Julie. Not only did she need the information, but her hope was that the conversation would ease both their minds.

"Forty-year-old man complained of cough and fever. Tested at 101.3. Confirmed that he had been out of the country in the last two weeks. I've already tasked one of the other nurses with trying to find out who all he came in contact with during that time. He lives alone and said he came in when it grew hard for him to breathe. I've taken a swab and sent it to the lab for analysis. Unfortunately, I guess this means I'm under quarantine until my test comes back."

Candace could hear the sadness in Julie's voice. She knew Julie had children at home. They were younger, and while her husband would be there, Candace couldn't imagine how hard it must be to know she couldn't go home to her kids.

Candace placed a gloved hand on Julie's arm. "Hey, it will be okay. We'll rush your test and you'll be home in no time. I'll handle everything else for him so that once you're cleared, you can go home, okay?"

Julie sucked in a deep breath and nodded. Candace did the same. Then she turned to the isolation door and entered the room into territory unknown.

Gabe flicked through the channels on the television mindlessly. It was how he had spent the majority of the last few months. With Melinda and the kids gone, he no longer knew what to do with himself. Having taken little time off over the years, he'd had quite the bank of sick days built up and had decided to cash them in. He knew he would be unable to focus on work, but he hadn't expected he'd be unable to focus on anything else as well.

When his phone vibrated beside him, he glanced at the screen and sighed. His boss. Though he did not want to talk to her, he couldn't afford to lose this job, and she probably wanted to know when he would be coming back. He didn't really have an answer, but he swiped the screen to take the call anyway.

"Hello?"

"Gabe?" Surprise colored her voice even through the phone, and he could almost picture her pinched forehead and arched brows. "Are you okay?"

What a question. Was he okay with the love of his life and his children gone? No. Was he okay with no answer as to where they went or who took them? No. Was he physically okay and able to take care of himself? That was debatable. "Define okay."

She sighed. "I'm sorry about your family, Gabe. We all lost someone in the disappearances, but I need you to come back to work."

"Why?"

"I'm sure you've heard on the news about the NCAV."

He had though he had paid little attention to it. What did it matter to him anyway?

"Well, we have a patient who tested positive in Washington state and we're receiving samples to analyze tomorrow. I need my best people on this, and you are one of the best."

A tiny spark of enthusiasm flickered in Gabe. It felt like it had been so long since something had interested him and studying the new virus *was* interesting. But was it interesting enough? He took a moment to look around the room. Discarded clothes and trash lay about the room and dirty dishes sat piled on the nearby tables. He hadn't even gathered the energy to take them to the kitchen. It was clear that something had to change. Perhaps feeling useful again would be it. He could throw himself into his work, and this time there would be no one to disappoint when he missed dinner or came home late.

"Okay," he said. "I'll be in tomorrow."

"Great. And Gabe? Clean up first."

He wasn't sure how she knew, but perhaps it was only an educated guess on her part. It certainly wouldn't have been a leap. "I will."

6

As Lily walked into the school two weeks later, the energy felt different. All around her, students were talking in hushed whispers, and there was an aura of fear that she'd never encountered before in the building. It floated like an invisible mist affecting everything it touched. She knew it was because of the rumors of a shut down. Though the President had claimed to have closed down the borders to outside travel over a month ago when the virus first hit the news, it evidently hadn't been quick enough. The mysterious virus that no one seemed to know much about had sneaked its way into the US and infected someone just two hours up the road in Seattle. That case had turned into ten and then quickly into hundreds. Though it appeared to only be infecting Seattle currently, the governor - whom Lily had cared little about until this point - now threatened to shut down schools and businesses across the state to slow the spread.

A part of Lily still believed that the virus wouldn't make it to Olympia. Seattle was a big city, crowded, with lots of people packed together in small spaces. More people rode transit buses than drove and many worked in cubicles crammed into small offices. It was prime real estate for any contagious disease, evidenced by its higher rate of annual flu cases, but Olympia was smaller, more spread out, protected. Still, she couldn't get the virus out of her mind.

Over the last week, she had begun researching everything she could about this virus. The media claimed it was highly contagious - some compared it to The Spanish Flu in the early 1900s. Not being a history buff, Lily then had to research The Spanish Flu. What she found had sent tremors of trepidation through her. Medical practices were not nearly as good in 1918, so that created a glimmer of hope, but it still appeared as if closing businesses and schools was one of the few things that slowed the spread back then. Though she knew it was irrational, she didn't want school to close.

"I heard Seattle is shutting down," Katie said, falling into step beside Lily. As usual, she passed her a coffee as they continued down the hall.

"Yeah, I heard. I really hope it doesn't come here."

Lily took a sip of the coffee and waited for the normal feeling of contentment to blanket her, but for once it did not have the usual warming effect.

"Me too."

"Dude, did you hear Seattle shut down their schools?" Though not speaking directly to them, Isaiah's excited voice carried across the room as they entered. "I hope we get to shut down." Isaiah was notorious for doing as little work as possible, so it came as no surprise that he would prefer to be out of school.

"Not me," Hannah said, organizing the books on her desk into a neat stack. "I'd like to actually get to graduate."

Isaiah rolled his eyes and waved his hands in a dismissive gesture. "We wouldn't close that long. Just a couple of weeks for them to clean everything. I could use two weeks of sleeping in and no homework."

"We'd have to make up the time," Hannah said as if speaking to a child instead of an eighteen-year-old boy. "I don't want to lose my summer."

Isaiah's face fell as if he hadn't considered that fact. "Okay, I don't want to go longer in the summer, but surely they'll forgive the days, right? Like snow days? Or give us packets to work on? That's what my friend up north is doing."

"Packets?" Katie nearly shouted. "That's not real learning."

He shrugged. "Better than going longer in the summer. That's my time off, man."

If the topic hadn't been so heavy, Lily might have rolled her eyes at Isaiah. He rarely turned work in as it was, so school time also seemed to be his time off.

The discussions continued as Lily sank into her seat, but they only enforced the sick feeling rumbling around in her stomach. She had thought this pandemic was interesting - as long as it stayed over in China or Europe, far away from her, but now that it was here and messing up her life, she just wanted it to go away.

True to form, Mr. Higgins began class by having the students share any new information they had learned about the virus, but Lily couldn't get into the conversation. She was thinking about everything that would change in her life if they got shut down. Would they close her gym? It had been forced to close for a few days months ago when all the people had disappeared because a car had smashed through the front entrance, but Brian had reopened as quickly as possible. Hitting the bag or mitts with a partner had been her sanity when everything else seemed crazy in the world. Now, she hated to miss class for any reason, and she couldn't imagine having to miss for two weeks. Especially if everything else closed as well. What would she do?

As first period ended and she gathered up her belongings, she couldn't help but feel that they were working on borrowed time. She moved in a daze to the next class, feeling like she was one of those banal characters in a horror movie just waiting for something to jump out and scare her.

The next class was English, which she normally loved. Mrs. Fox was her favorite teacher. Not only did she make learning more fun with her random accents and crazy stories, but she always told the students information straight. They all knew that though other teachers would hedge around the answers, Mrs. Fox would tell them what she could, and Lily loved that she treated the students more like equals, at least when possible.

Sliding into her desk, she pulled out her copy of Frankenstein. They had just begun reading the novel, and she was enjoying the book. Mostly. Parts were definitely boring, but it was interesting to see how well Mary Shelley wrote for someone of her age. Somewhere, back in the deep recesses of her mind, Lily often wondered if she had what it took to be a writer. She'd dabbled in creating stories as a child and she used to read a ton, but somewhere along the way, writing had fallen to the side.

Before Mrs. Fox could even begin class, the loudspeaker crackled, and Lily's stomach knotted. Somehow, she knew what was coming next.

"Sorry for the interruption, students." The principal's voice sounded calm, but it did nothing to alleviate the bunching in her stomach. "Due to the governor's mandate, we will be closing the school for the next two weeks. Please be sure to grab what you might need for that time frame before you leave today. Your teachers will have more information."

Silence descended on the room as all eyes turned toward Mrs. Fox. Her smile appeared pinched and forced as she gazed out at the room. "Okay, you guys all know how to access Google Classroom." They'd spent the last few days getting familiarized with the system just in case, but Lily had hoped it would remain a "just in case" scenario.

"I'll be putting assignments up there starting on Wednesday. The staff will be taking a few days to gather and decide on the best path going forward, but then we'll hit the ground running. Reading Frankenstein long distance isn't the way I had planned to do it, but we can make it work. So, be sure to take your book and your packets home."

Everyone around Lily began gathering up their supplies, but she shuffled to the front of the room where the teacher stood, a smile still pasted on her face. "Mrs. Fox, do you think we'll be back in two weeks?"

When her lips mashed together and her eyes darted from one side to the other, Lily could tell that she was trying to decide how much to say. Finally, she sighed, and Lily knew she was going to get the truth. At least the truth as Mrs. Fox knew it. "I hope so, Lily, but I kind of doubt it.

If this virus is spreading the way they say it is, I can't imagine that we'll be back in school in just two weeks."

Though it was not what she wanted to hear, Lily knew she was right. Every discussion in Mr. Higgins' class supported those words, but she didn't want to hear them. "I don't want to end the year this way."

Mrs. Fox placed a comforting hand on her shoulder. "No one does, Lily, but we just have to have a little faith that everything will be okay."

Faith wasn't something Lily had employed for a while. Her family had once attended church, but when her parents' careers took off, Sundays became a day of resting from the long week and nothing else. Then, after the disappearances, most churches closed. Perhaps it was time to find faith again. Holding back the tears pricking her eyes, Lily nodded. She returned to her desk, gathered up her things, and shoved them in her backpack. Then, she joined the throng of students flowing out of the room and toward their lockers to grab any other last-minute items.

By noon, Lily was home. Alone. With nothing to do. Her father was an attorney and didn't normally arrive home until after six most nights. Her mother worked at an insurance office and was generally out until five, and her siblings were both older and out of the house already. With time to kill, she opened her laptop and began poring over articles again. How long could this shutdown last? Not forever, right?

Raven's breath caught as she watched the news conference. Across the US, states were shutting down schools and businesses in an effort to "flatten the curve." At least, that's what they claimed. The idea made no sense to Raven. Unless everything shut down, which wasn't possible as people would still need food and gas and other necessities like that, then those people who had to continue working would still spread the disease and when the economy opened up again, the cases would simply increase once more. It felt like a Band-Aid instead of a solution, and Raven wondered where the common sense had gone.

The image of her governor filled the screen, and Raven's hand flew to her mouth. It had been so long since she'd seen them that she had begun to wonder if they'd been a dream, but there behind the most important man in Washington state was a dark shadow. Why was she seeing them again now? And what did one behind the governor mean?

Raven jumped from the couch and retrieved her laptop from her desk. After signing in, she took a deep breath and placed her fingers on the keys. She was about to do something she hadn't done in a long time. She was going to enter the dark web.

The dark web was not a place she went often. When

she was young, its taboo name and reputation had lured her to find it, but once there, she'd been appalled by some of the things she found. Coming from an abusive house herself, she'd been sickened by posts requesting children as if they were property. Raven knew what would happen to those kids if they got delivered to the sick requesters and it was nothing good. Briefly, she wondered if those kinds of posts had fallen away after most children under the age of five and many under the age of ten had disappeared.

At first, Raven hadn't quite understood why some children had been left behind, but she'd managed to find something about the age of accountability in Kat's journal. It was as close to an explanation as she could get - some kids reached it faster than others and those who reached it had faced the same opportunity to accept God as she had. They had either accepted Him and been taken with the others or rejected Him and been left behind.

Shaking her head to clear the rabbit trail, she focused back on the task at hand. While the dark web was a hangout for sickos and weirdos, it was also where confidential information sometimes lived. Information that the government didn't want to get out. And that was what she was searching for.

She began by typing in NCAV though she didn't think it would be that easy. She was right. A few posts appeared, but they were mainly conspiracy theories about how aliens were behind this. Shaking her head, she scoffed lightly at how aliens seemed to be the catchall for anything not easily explained. She supposed she had once been one of those people, but she wondered now how people could believe in aliens and not believe in God.

Her fingers tapped at the keys as she chewed on her bottom lip. What should she be searching for? Fault? A coverup? What? Suddenly, the image of patient zero filled her mind. He'd been a lab technician in China, but he'd been unable to explain how he'd been infected. In fact, he'd claimed there was a period of time that seemed to be blank for him, though the media had dismissed it as a symptom of the virus. What had his name been?

Liu Wei Chang. Like a firework, the image of his name flashed in front of her eyes, and her fingers quickly typed the correct keys. Dozens of stories filled her screen. She clicked on the first one and scanned it, her fear increasing as she did.

Liu Wei Chang had been seen being pulled into a vehicle the morning of the day he appeared to not remember, yet his employer claimed he'd been at work the entire day. Even more disturbing was the fact that the woman who reported the abduction turned up dead a week later, supposedly from the virus.

Liu, though he had recovered from NCAV, had been placed on medical leave after continuing to speak out about his memory loss and was now being treated at a psychiatric hospital. His family members had disappeared.

Raven blinked at the screen, unsure of what to make of this. Was this some crazy conspiracy theory or was there some nefarious play occurring that no one knew about? Though not prone to follow crazy theories, Kat's words continued to rattle around in her head.

Could this virus have been planned to allow some savior to rise to power? And if so, were the US leaders accomplices or were they simply pawns in the game being played?

Though she knew Candace wouldn't have all the answers, Raven also knew she was on the front lines and would at least be able to verify what the media was saying. Hoping that she wouldn't be busy at the moment, Raven dialed Candace's number.

"Hello?" Candace's voice sounded breathless on the other end.

"Is it as bad as they're saying?" Raven decided to forgo the pleasantries; she knew Candace had caller ID and would know it was her.

"Yes and no. Hold on a second." There was a pause, a shuffling noise, and when Candace came back on the line, her voice was much quieter. "It doesn't appear to be as deadly as the media is claiming, but it is certainly contagious. We are working twenty-four hour shifts here without much of a break, but so far, we've only lost about ten patients and all of them were over the age of seventy."

"What happens to the younger patients?"

"For some, it's little more than flu-like symptoms. A few have come in needing breathing treatments, but generally they're released in a few days. Something weird is going on though."

"What's that?" This whole thing felt weird to Raven, like something out of a sci-fi movie, but she had a bad feeling it was something she would get used to.

"We've been giving patients this drug called Ramidil. Basically, it just boosts the immune system to help recognize and fight the cytokine storm that some of the severe patients we're seeing here have."

"Okay, pretend I understand all that," Raven said, jotting down notes to research later. "What's going on with it?"

Candace's voice dropped to a whisper. "Well, it's been helping the patients we've been giving it to, but now we're getting orders not to use it."

"What? Why?"

"I don't know. Look, I have to go, but I'll try to get down Sunday, okay?"

"Okay, stay safe and keep me in the loop."

"Will do."

Raven stared at her phone for a minute. What did all this mean? The virus wasn't as deadly as the media was saying, at least from Candace's viewpoint, so why spread that it was? Fear was the only answer, but why keep the people in fear? And why stop a treatment that could help people? It looked like Raven was going to have to spend a lot more time in the dark web.

She'd just put in a search for Ramidil when a knock sounded at her front door, sending her jumping and quickly backtracking out of the dark web, erasing her footprint as she did. It was doubtful someone was onto her already, but she had no idea if anything she'd been looking into was dangerous or not.

After closing the laptop and placing it on the coffee table, she crossed to the door and opened it to find Jason standing on the other side. She knew him well enough by now to know that the long expression he currently wore did not mean good news.

"Jason, what's the matter?" she asked as she ushered him into her living room.

"I think I'm about to be unemployed," he said, his shoulders dropping.

"Yeah, I heard." Jason worked part time as a bartender and part time at Brian's gym as an instructor, but with schools closing, he must assume, like Raven did, that bars and gyms wouldn't be far behind. Raven hoped he would want to do more with his life one day, but she could see that the gym was his passion, and he had confided to her that he was hoping that Brian would leave it to him when he retired.

"What am I going to do if they close, Raven?" he

asked as he plopped down on her couch. "I don't have much money saved up."

Actually, that was probably an exaggeration. Though she cared for Jason, maybe even loved him, he had an awful habit of spending money as soon as he got it, sometimes even before he got it. She'd heard him ask Brian for a draw a few times, and he'd even borrowed money from her a handful of times though he had appeared to be making progress on that area the last few months.

Raven sat down beside him and placed a hand on his arm. "We'll figure it out, but I'm worried, Jason. I think this may only be the beginning."

"What do you mean?"

"Let me show you." Raven grabbed her laptop and pulled up the information she had been looking into before. "Remember patient zero?"

"Yeah, what about him?"

"He's in a psych hospital now and his family has disappeared." She pointed to the story as if indicating he should read it.

"Okay, that's a little weird, but it could all be coincidental," Jason said slowly.

Normally, she liked that he didn't jump to conclusions, but this time it was important he understood what this might mean. "Right, but remember how he claimed there was a part of his day he couldn't remember and the doctors all claimed it was a symptom of the virus?" Jason nodded, but it was clear he still wasn't following. "Well, there was also a woman who claims to have seen him taken that morning. She came forward and days later, she wound up dead."

"Okay, we're getting into a weird category now," Jason admitted. "What are you thinking?"

Raven held up a finger before grabbing Kat's letter from the coffee table and holding it out to him. "Honestly, I'm thinking this."

An expression of exasperation that she'd rarely seen cross Jason's features contorted his face now. "Raven, not this again."

"I'm serious, Jason. When I was watching the news about this virus last week, I felt like maybe it was something more, and I was reminded of Kat's letter. She said hard times were coming and they could be anything. Anything that would send people looking for a savior. Plus, I just got off the phone with Candace." While Jason hadn't officially met Candace as Raven hadn't convinced him to join her at church yet, she had spoken of the woman often. "She told me that they're being told not to use a treatment that appears to be working. She also said that the virus doesn't seem as deadly as the media is claiming."

"Okay, but what does that have to do with Kat's letter?"

"What if this virus, the media coverage, all of it, what

if it's to create enough fear that people begin to look for a savior? What if this is the beginning of the end she spoke about?"

Jason shook his head and sighed. "I don't know, Raven. We went down this path before, after she left, remember? And we came up empty."

Raven placed her hand on his knee. She knew that nothing had seemed to happen right after the disappearances. At least nothing like "the tribulation." "I know, but what if it was because the time wasn't right?"

Jason's brows knitted together. "The time wasn't right? Everything had fallen apart; how could the time not have been right?"

Raven wasn't exactly sure what she meant. It was just something that had been tugging at her brain. "Kat told me once that God worked in His own time. I didn't start seeing the dark shapes until Kat came into my life, and maybe that was so I would believe her. Then they left, or at least I stopped seeing them, but maybe that was because whatever was being set in motion hadn't happened yet. I think I saw one again today. Behind the governor at the press conference."

"Okay," Jason said with a sigh, "Let's say that's the case. What are we supposed to do about it?"

"Yeah," Raven bit her lip again, "I still haven't figured that part out yet." She'd been posting videos weekly on the TruthSeeker site, and she knew people were watching them and finding local churches, but she felt like she should be doing more. But what?

Gabe Cross looked up from his microscope and motioned his associate over. "Look at this."

"What am I looking at?" she asked, pushing up her thick black glasses. Celia was no supermodel in the looks department, but she was smart - the smartest associate he'd ever worked with.

"I don't want to tell you yet. You just tell me what you see." He hoped he was wrong. He was tired after all, having spent the last two months in a deep depression over the loss of his family and the last two weeks working nearly nonstop studying the NCAV. The first few samples they had received had been too small or too damaged to see much. Thankfully, or perhaps unfortunately depending on how one looked at it, there were now many more cases of NCAV in the states which meant more samples to analyze.

Celia lifted an eyebrow but obliged his wish and leaned into the microscope. "Whoa, what is that?"

So, he wasn't going crazy. Gabe ran a hand through his dark hair and sighed. "I'm not sure, but that doesn't look like any natural virus I've ever seen."

She pushed back from the microscope and chewed on

her lip. "No, it doesn't, but what are we going to do about it?"

"We have to tell someone, right? Everything I've heard is that they think this came from an animal, but this proves that's not true. Won't that change the way we need to combat it?"

"Maybe, but…" her eyes shifted to the floor and she twisted her hands together in her lap. The moment of silence dragged out until she finally looked back up at him. "Did you lose anyone in the disappearances?"

Gabe tensed as if she'd pulled a knife on him instead of posing a simple question. Yes, he'd lost someone, three someones to be exact. The love of his life and his two children. He never spoke of them anymore though they plagued his thoughts constantly. He still wondered what had actually happened to them. The only scenario that seemed to fit was the one that sounded craziest to most people - the rapture. He knew Melinda had attended church as had his kids, but he'd attended church with them on occasion, so why would he have been left behind? Perhaps it was his scientific mind - the mind that had grappled with the idea of God's existence and now grappled with the thought that God had taken his family away.

"I can see by your expression that you did," she said, continuing, "I'm not surprised. I think almost everyone did. I lost my whole family."

"I'm sorry, but what does that have to do with this?"

Gabe didn't mean to sound heartless, but he didn't want to hear her story or reopen his own wounds. It would do neither of them any good.

"Do you remember how after they first disappeared, some people were claiming it was due to the rapture?"

Gabe would never admit it, but though many dismissed it as rubbish, he still found it the most plausible explanation. "Yeah."

"Well, do you remember what happened to those people?" She pushed up her glasses and stared pointedly at him.

Suddenly, he understood where she was going. "They were labeled as crazy people."

"Not only labeled. They were vilified and discredited. Some of them will probably never get a job again. I'm not saying we shouldn't say something eventually, but we need to think about the best way first. I don't know about you, but I'd like to keep my job."

As would he. It was all he had left, really. "Okay, we'll sit on it. For now." But Gabe wondered how long he could agree. He might have a lot of faults, but integrity was one thing he prided himself on, and the churning in his gut told him he wouldn't be able to stay silent for long.

✽ 7 ✽

"I'm sorry, sir. The virus isn't quite as deadly as we'd hoped." Fear billowed around the demon who cowered before Samael and Daman, and his eyes stayed glued to the ground as if he was afraid even looking in their eyes would mean instant death.

"And why is that?" Daman asked. He'd wanted the virus to be a force, to run through the population at will, so that no one felt safe, but now this man was telling him otherwise.

"I'm not sure, sir. The scientists have said that it might be that some people already had immunity to part of the strain they used to modify it. Evidently, they had to pull from old viruses to make something that would work. And it is still working," he added quickly as if to soften the blow. "The elderly are hit especially hard as well as anyone with immune disorders. It just isn't affecting the young and healthy in quite the same way."

"I see." Part of Daman wanted to rip the demon to shreds right then. He did not like being disappointed, but perhaps there was a way to play up what they could. "You say the elderly are affected?"

"Yes, sir." The demon finally lifted his eyes as if sensing the change in Daman's demeanor.

"And humans love their elders, correct?" Daman stroked his chin as he ran through scenarios in his mind.

"Most do, yes."

"So, most would do anything to try and save them?" Pieces were falling into place for Daman. If the deaths alone didn't break them, maybe he could find another way.

"I suppose so." The demon glanced to Samael as if looking for a clue as to what Daman was thinking.

"What would inconvenience them to the point that they'd be willing to do anything to get back to quote normal?" Daman flicked his bony fingers in the gesture of quotation marks that he had seen the humans do time and again.

"Besides the lockdowns? Most places are shutting down businesses to try and stop the disease."

"Not all places though," Daman said quickly. "Make sure they leave the right places open. Abortion clinics, bars, drug shops, anything that appeals to the base nature of humans. Those must be allowed to continue."

"Of course, sir," the demon said, bowing again.

"Now, what else can we do to make life unbearable for most? If we can't make the disease worse, can we at least make the cure unbearable? At least until I step in with the real cure?"

The demon cocked his head as if thinking back through the years. "In 1918 when what they called The Spanish Flu hit, doctors required people to quarantine and wear masks. The people agreed for a time, but eventually, they revolted. Is that something along what you are thinking, sir?"

"Possibly," Daman tapped his fingers on the edge of his throne, "but we don't want any revolts. How long might we have before a revolt might occur?"

"It was over a year in 1918, sir."

"A year. That would give us long enough to come up with a cure, correct?" He probably wouldn't even need the whole year, especially as some of the humans were still suffering due to the rapture.

The demon paled. "From what I understand, no cure has ever been created so quickly. They might be fearful of it."

"Then we must convince them not to be afraid or find ways to force them to accept it. Go, tell the others to spread the word that not only should lockdowns continue, but masks should be worn. Lay the seeds for a cure. It's time the world began to learn the name Daman Caturix."

"This can't be happening," Brian growled from his desk.

Raven stopped her workout and glanced over at Jason who was scrawling boxing combos on the portable white board they kept at the front of the gym. She'd come in a little early to work out, so it was just the three of them in the room at the moment, but Brian's anger radiated out in waves and seemed to fill the entire space. Even before she asked, Raven knew what he held in his hand. "What is it, Brian?"

"A cease-and-desist order. Evidently, the governor, in 'an effort to flatten the curve'," he said in a mocking voice, "is forcing all non-essential businesses to shut down for two weeks."

Jason's eyes caught hers as they approached Brian's desk. They'd both felt this was coming, but actually having it happen was another matter.

"Is that legal? Can he even do that?" Anger colored Brian's voice and sent a chill down Raven's spine. She had never seen him this angry, not even when he'd had to replace the front of the building. "Doesn't the constitution grant life, liberty, and the pursuit of happiness? How is forcing me to close my business not stealing my liberty and pursuit of happiness?"

Raven shook her head. "I don't know, but you're right about the constitution. Evidently, he's claiming some emergency powers that enable him to make some of these rules - closing schools, businesses. I don't know how it can be legal, but I can ask around."

Brian threw down the letter and dropped his head in his hands. Raven knew he wasn't mad at them but at the situation. She hadn't been a member of the gym long, but she'd grown close to both Brian and Jason since joining and she'd heard Brian's story.

This gym was his baby. A former police officer, he'd always had a passion for kickboxing and karate. When he'd saved up enough money that he could afford equipment, he'd retired from the force and opened the gym. It had started in his garage at first, but soon, he'd garnered enough clients that he'd been able to rent an old warehouse. It was large and dusty half the time, but it was like his second home. Even his wife had joined in, teaching classes in the afternoons.

"This is ridiculous," he said, glancing up from the paper. "How can liquor and pot shops be deemed essential but gyms not? Don't they understand how important exercise is to health?"

Raven shook her head again, but deep down, she thought she knew the answer - it was because liquor and pot shops paid a hefty fee to the government while gyms and other small businesses didn't. Shutting liquor stores and pot shops down would drain the government's money quickly, but shutting down smaller businesses like Brian's, even for a short time, would put people out of work. Since the working people paid taxes and the taxes funded government, Raven still didn't understand how they could keep them closed for long. What would the government do without all their tax dollars?

Jason ran a hand across his chin. "It's only two weeks, right? Can we make it the two weeks?"

Brian sighed and scratched at the side of his face before meeting Jason's eyes. "If it's only two weeks, yes, but if it goes longer than that," he shook his head, "I don't know how I can keep paying you."

Raven felt like an awkward third wheel in the conversation, but she also knew she couldn't stay silent. "Don't worry, Brian. We'll figure something out." She had no idea what, but she wasn't going to let the state destroy the two people she had grown closest to in the last few months. There had to be something they could do.

8

Though Raven's job was generally solitary, she, like nearly everyone else in the state, had received word that for the foreseeable future, she would be performing her duties from her own living room instead of the office. While Raven didn't miss the annoying noise of her coworkers, she was beginning to feel a little stir-crazy. There was almost nothing to do now as it appeared nearly everything in the state was shutting down. Everything except grocery stores, gas stations, pot shops, liquor stores, and abortion clinics which were all somehow deemed essential. Some people were able to work from home, like herself, but many others like Jason were now unemployed and unsure where their next check was coming from. With a sigh, Raven grabbed her jacket and headed outside for a quick walk. At least walking outside was still allowed, and maybe the fresh air would clear her mind.

She'd lived in her neighborhood for years, but she couldn't remember the last time she'd walked the streets during the day. Everything felt quiet and odd. With nearly everything shut down, shouldn't more people be outside?

Raven turned down the side street that led to a small park. Goosebumps had erupted on her arms, and she suddenly just wanted to see other people. Surely, some of the older kids who were out of school would be in the field or even playing on the equipment, but the park was empty.

However, someone had been there recently. Near the entrance was a sign staked in the ground. Raven moved closer to read it. *Park closed due to NCAV spread.* Closed? How did one even close a park? Then her eyes landed on the yellow caution tape surrounding the play structure.

Not only had the governor shut down schools, but he'd shut down playgrounds as well? True, there were fewer kids now than six months ago due to the disappearances - and those children would already need therapy in the future - but now they weren't even able to play outside and try to find some semblance of normality again? What did the future hold for them?

Though no one was around her, Raven felt a tremor of fear snake its way up her spine, and she turned back toward her house. Suddenly, being stir-crazy in her house seemed more appealing than being outside.

Anger boiled inside Lily as she watched the governor give his latest press conference. It seemed he was only capable of doling out bad news. Not only had he extended the lockdowns for another month, but he'd also just shut down schools for the rest of the year.

"Can you believe him?" Lily asked Katie as she muted the TV. She had no desire to hear the news anchors pontificate about how caring the governor was being, especially since he'd just destroyed her hope for a normal end of the school year.

She supposed deep down she had assumed that would be the case, but she'd been hoping the temporary lockdown would be just that - temporary - and they would get to go back. Online school was not nearly as fun as being in class. It was odd. Lily could remember complaining everyday about having to get up and go to school, but now she wanted nothing more than to have that freedom.

Katie sighed and pushed herself up from the couch. "I hate how he applies the same standard for the whole state as he does for those with the higher case count. The last time I checked, we only had five cases in our whole county."

Lily stood and followed her into the kitchen. "Right? Like why can't we finish school?"

Katie chuckled as she opened the cabinet and grabbed a bag of popcorn. "You just want to go back because you're hoping The Spring Fling will be rescheduled."

She wasn't wrong about that. Bryce had barely even returned Lily's text messages since the shutdown, and she was eager to see him again. Plus, she really wanted to dance with him. Heat crawled up her neck and flamed across her cheeks as she imagined his arms wrapped around her. "Okay, true. I want to go to the dance first and foremost, but you can't tell me you are enjoying this distance learning thing."

Katie shrugged and turned on the microwave. "I don't know. It's not that bad. I feel like they're giving us less work than if we were in school which gives me more time to research what I want, but I do miss being able to go out. You know I haven't gotten to get a coffee in weeks."

"I haven't done anything in weeks," Lily said, folding her arms across her chest. "Do you think we'll ever get to go back to normal?"

Katie shook her head. Clearly it was a question she had no answer for either. "Who knows, but speaking of normal, have you been to the grocery store recently?"

Grocery stores, gas stations, liquor stores, and pot shops were about the only places the governor had deemed as essential to stay open, and Lily and Katie were only old enough to enter two of the four. Every other business had been ordered to shutter its doors until further notice. Even doctor's offices had canceled appointments and were only seeing emergency cases.

Katie had switched subjects so abruptly that Lily blinked at her for a few moments before answering. "Not in a few days. Why?"

"People are starting to wear masks in the grocery store. Not the workers or anything, but shoppers. Haven't the doctors been saying not to wear masks?"

Lily shrugged as the popcorn began popping in the microwave behind Katie. "People are paranoid. I guess whatever makes them feel better." When the virus had first hit, she'd watched the news daily, hoping for some good news that they had it under control and life could continue as normal. Unfortunately, that hadn't happened, and now it was generally a repeat of the same things: wash your hands, stay home, stay away from people. She was tired of hearing it.

"I'm not wearing any mask," she continued. Lily couldn't stand things around her neck or her face. Turtleneck sweaters never even touched her body because she felt like they were choking her. Having something blocking her ability to breathe in clean air sounded like torture.

"What if he passes a mask mandate?" Katie leveled a serious gaze at Lily. "They have in China and many of the other countries."

"Yeah, but they have way more cases than we do. We only have five, right?"

The popping stopped, and Katie opened the microwave. "Five can become fifty pretty quickly."

Lily scoffed. "Even fifty would be small here. Our county has over two hundred and fifty thousand people."

Katie opened the bag and poured the popcorn into a bowl. Steam and a sweet salty smell filled the air. "I don't know. I just have a bad feeling about all of this."

Though Katie had bad feelings about a lot of things, Lily couldn't dismiss this one so easily. She too had a feeling that things were going to get much worse before they got better.

"You up for that movie?" Katie asked.

Lily nodded, but she wondered if she'd be able to concentrate with everything circling in her head.

Candace Markham glanced up at Dr. Aikens. "I'm sorry, we're supposed to do what?"

"Label the patient as an NCAV fatality if they die and test positive for the virus." He repeated the statement as if he couldn't believe she hadn't understood the first time, but she couldn't believe what he was asking them to do.

"I'm sorry, but I need to get this straight. If someone comes in with a gunshot wound-"

"You test them for NCAV," he said, interrupting her. "We test everyone that comes in."

"Okay, so we test this person, and for argument's sake, let's assume they have the virus, but it's the gunshot wound that kills them, we're still supposed to list it as an NCAV fatality?"

"Yes. Look," he heaved an enormous sigh, "the hospital receives twice as much money for a death labeled an NCAV death as it does for a routine death, so…" He spread his hands as if that should satisfy her.

Candace glanced around at the other doctors at the table. A few stared back at her, but most had their faces glued to the table as if they'd rather be anywhere else right now. "So, we're going to lie to the government and the people? For money?"

"The hospital needs the money," he said. "The government is offering it. We're simply playing by their rules."

"But doesn't anyone care why the government is offering more money for this? What's the point of inflating the death numbers?" But suddenly she knew. The lock-downs. Across the US, governors had declared that all non-essential businesses and schools shut down for two weeks to "slow the spread." The point had been to keep the hospitals from being overrun with patients as those in Italy had been, and Candace had been all for that, but this? This made it feel as if there was an ulterior motive.

As if maybe two weeks wasn't the plan at all, but then she should have guessed that when the governor extended the lockdown another two weeks and closed the schools for the rest of the year.

People were already scared of this virus because no one seemed to know much about it. Hand sanitizer and cleaning products were flying off the shelves faster than stores could re-shelve them, which made sense, but so were toilet paper and canned goods. It was like people were expecting to be locked down in their homes for months instead of weeks, and inflating the death numbers would only cause more fear and panic.

However, Candace could see that perhaps it would also create complacency. People who normally wouldn't stay home because they valued their freedom might if they thought the virus was worse than it actually was. And from what Candace had personally seen, that was the case. Yes, they had lost patients, but most of them had been elderly and suffering from poor immune systems before they were exposed to the virus. She had yet to see anyone under the age of fifty succumb to the virus personally, and across the country the deaths for those under the age of twenty were microscopic. So, why exactly were schools closed?

"This is wrong," she muttered under her breath, but she stopped herself from saying more. Though it tore at the empathetic, truthful part of her, a small part of her thought that perhaps she could learn more by staying on the inside, by being close to the action. If she made a ruckus now, they would just fire her. Better to stay quiet and see if there really was something nefarious going on or if perhaps the government, in its infinite wisdom, had truly thought they were going to help hospitals facing the crisis instead of encouraging false numbers.

"It's what we've been required to do," the supervisor continued, "and we will follow orders. Is that understood?" He glanced around the room, but he stared longest at Candace.

"Understood," she mumbled along with the rest of the doctors in the room. She would play along and follow orders. For now.

"Now, let's discuss protective equipment. There's been some new guidelines on those as well, and we are working as hard as we can to get enough of the correct equipment for everyone. Dr. Goodman, the head of infectious diseases, had been telling people not to wear masks in order to save them for front line workers, but now he is recommending masks for everybody which means that even though he says N95 masks should be saved for those of us dealing with the disease closely, people will buy them up. We've all seen the empty shelves-"

As he continued, Candace nodded as if she was listening, but her mind was already wandering. What did all of this have to do with the tribulation?

✠ 9 ✠

"Due to Dr. Goodman's new statement that masks help reduce the spread of NCAV, I am requiring that all businesses in the state of Washington require masks to enter."

Raven rolled her eyes and shook her head as she watched Governor Smythe give his most recent press conference. The media, including the sainted Dr. Goodman, had spent the last few months telling everyone not to wear masks, and now all of a sudden, they were required? What had changed? Because it surely wasn't the science behind it.

"I know this is an inconvenience for people as are the business closures, but hopefully this will allow us to open more of those businesses soon. In a limited capacity, of course."

Governor Smythe continued to drone on for a few more minutes, opining about how concerned he was for everyone's health. Raven was just about to turn the television off when a banner flashed across the screen that breaking news was coming up. She decided to wait and see what the breaking news might be.

As soon as Governor Smythe disappeared from the screen, the regular news anchor appeared. "It's been quite a trying time for our state over the last few months. Total cases are now in the thousands with deaths in the hundreds, but we do have some good news to report. A foreign businessman by the name of Daman Caturix has stepped into the limelight, promising to back the productions of masks and research for a vaccine, so that we can all get back to normal. Let's listen to what he has to say."

The screen switched to a pale man with dark hair, dark eyes, and bony features that sent a chill racing down Raven's spine. Even his close-lipped smile evoked a sense of revulsion in her stomach, but when he began to speak, she knew she was looking at pure evil.

"You have probably never heard of me. My name is Daman Caturix, and until recently, I have lived a quiet life. However, I have been watching the devastation that this virus is creating, and I can no longer remain silent. I know that I am more fortunate than some, and I want to use that fortune to help as many people as I can. Among other businesses, I own a manufacturing plant and I have asked them to begin making masks and sending them out to any company who requests them. In addition, I have begun speaking with the largest medical research labs and will be donating whatever capital they need to create a cure for this virus as soon as possible. Though we are asked to distance right now, we can work together to achieve this new normal."

New normal? Raven wanted nothing to do with any kind of new normal. She rather liked the old normal, and something about this man sent every hair on her body standing at attention. It was time to see exactly who Daman Caturix was.

"Seriously? Masks are now required?" Lily turned off the television and tossed the remote to the side in disgust. She was so tired of this already. With no need to get up for school and little to do outside of her house, the days had soon lost their meaning. She couldn't even remember the last time she'd changed out of her pajamas into real clothes. Oh, she still showered daily, but instead of throwing on jeans and a top, she simply grabbed another pair of pajamas, and why not? It wasn't like anyone was going to see her.

Her father's office had been closed, but he was still working. Mainly in his bedroom with the door closed, the cell phone glued to his ear, and the computer open less than a foot away. She almost felt like she saw less of him now even though he was in the same house with her all day.

Her mother wasn't much better. Her office had transitioned to working at home as well which meant that she was now fielding calls from the house and then looking up the information she needed on the laptop. The woman shuffled around with a headset on, randomly spouting out, "Thank you for calling Insureman, how can I help you?" in between other tasks.

Both generally left her alone until noon when her mother would take a break from work, pop her head in Lily's room and ask about her school work. Lily normally had it all done by then as the teachers had assigned much less work than she would have done in school. While she welcomed the break, she also couldn't help but feel like she was getting cheated out of her education. Sometimes, her teachers would schedule Zoom meetings, but they were mostly just to answer questions, and Lily didn't have any. The majority of the work was simply reading an article or watching a video and answering a few questions with a paper thrown in here and there. Even if she didn't watch the video, she could search the answers quickly enough online.

The end of the school year was approaching, and it would end without fanfare. Everything had been canceled including The Spring Fling dance and graduation. Bryce had slipped out of her life, due to the virus or something else, she didn't know, and around the town, businesses were closing their doors forever in record numbers. Now, with the new mask mandate, there would be even fewer places to go as Lily held reservations about masks.

Most of her reservations came from the fact that for the last few months, every doctor on TV had been saying masks wouldn't help and people needed to not wear masks. Now, they were saying the exact opposite, but as far as Lily could tell, nothing had changed. They certainly weren't sharing any data that backed up this new claim. In addition, she didn't understand how breathing her own carbon dioxide could be good. She couldn't stand smelling other people's breath, so she was pretty sure she wouldn't like smelling her own all day either. It appeared outings to get groceries were even on hold for now. Unless she did the pickup option that allowed her to buy online and have someone bring the groceries out to her car.

Bored and frustrated, Lily picked up her phone and scrolled through her contacts. There weren't many left she could call. When school first let out, everyone had been agreeable to wanting to get together, but as the lockdowns continued, more and more of her friends began locking themselves inside their houses out of fear. Katie had told her that one of their friends had even refused to visit her grandfather on his birthday for fear she might be sick and not know it and give the virus to him. How had the media managed to convince healthy people they were dangerous so quickly?

Even the few who would still meet up required that it be outdoors and that everyone remain at least six feet from each other. Only Katie remained constant. A few times a week, the two would meet up and jog around the neighborhood.

Lily didn't enjoy running as much as she enjoyed hitting the bag at the gym, but it was still closed with no end in sight, so running had taken its place. In fact, that's what she needed to do today. Get out and run off her anger and clear her head.

She fired off a quick text to Katie asking if she wanted to join and then changed into workout wear while she waited for a reply. Her phone beeped as she pulled her hair into a ponytail.

Still working, but swing by when you're done and I can do a quick walk.

Lily sighed as she texted back a reply. Maybe it was a good thing though. Her pace was always a little slower when Katie ran with her, and today she needed to run out her frustrations. She grabbed her earbuds and headed downstairs to tell her mother where she was going.

Like normal, her mother was on the phone, so Lily scrawled a quick note and held it up for her mother to read. After a quick glance, her mother flashed a thumbs up sign, and Lily headed for the front door, turning on her music as she went.

The run started well, and Lily enjoyed the rhythm of her feet pounding on the pavement along with the beat in her ear, but as she passed the park a half mile from her house, a chill ran down her spine. The park had been roped off with yellow caution tape for as long as Lily had been out of school, so she wasn't sure why it was affecting her now. Once, someone had torn down the tape and Lily had hoped that meant the restrictions were easing, but the tape was back the next day. Maybe that was it. Maybe this lifeless park was a symbol for life as she knew it from now on.

Shaking her head to try and dispel the gloom that suddenly surrounded her, Lily turned her music up louder and decided she was ready to see Katie.

"Whoa, are you okay?" Katie asked when she opened the door.

"I don't know," Lily said. It was weird, but she still couldn't shake the depressed feeling that had cloaked her at the park. It was like it had marked her somehow and was following her wherever she went. "I ran by the park, and it just felt weird. The empty swings and the structures all taped off. I know it's been that way for weeks, so I don't know why it bothered me today, but it did."

Katie nodded and led the way to her room. "I understand. That park being empty of kids really shook me up after the disappearances, but now it feels almost sinister or something. I don't even know why the park is closed. Haven't they been saying that the virus couldn't be spread outside and that it didn't live long on surfaces?"

Lily chuffed as she sat on Katie's bed and folded one leg beneath her. No matter what channel one watched, the rules and regulations behind what the virus did and how they should combat it changed daily, but those two points had remained relatively constant. "Yeah, they did say that, but it seems that doesn't matter anymore. They also said masks wouldn't help and now the governor is mandating them. I don't know. Everything just feels off."

Katie sat against the headboard and pulled her knees to her chest. "You know what? You're right. It does feel off. They also said the shutdowns were only to flatten the curve, but we haven't had a week with more than five positive cases, so exactly what curve are we flattening?"

"Exactly," Lily said, sitting a little straighter. She wasn't prone to conspiracies, but there had been questions circling her mind for a while now. Ones that the media and government didn't seem to be able to or want to answer. "So, our hospitals aren't overcrowded and haven't been at any point. Do you think this is a power grab by the government?"

Lily hadn't known much about the governor until recently, but what she knew now did nothing to improve his image in her eyes. From everything she'd seen, he seemed to care more about climate change than anything else and routinely spent thousands of dollars trying to save a snail but openly supported the killing of babies in abortion. Still, she couldn't understand why he would want to decimate the state on purpose. Thousands were now out of work, and the unemployment numbers and payouts just kept rising.

Katie was silent for a moment, her lips mashed together. "Do you remember when we read 1984 and how we didn't understand at first why the government felt the need to rewrite history and things like that?"

Lily nodded. She hadn't made the connection before, but suddenly life felt a lot like 1984.

Katie continued, "I don't understand the government's purpose for keeping us locked down yet, but I feel like we are living in those times."

"I don't know if we've gone that far. Yet. But I am tired of all this shut down."

"I think we might be." Katie's voice was soft, almost hesitant. "Did you hear the governor state that people should just do drive-thru church services? I don't think he's ever been to a church service. Can you imagine a pastor giving a sermon like a hundred times?"

Lily's forehead wrinkled in confusion. "There are still churches? I thought they died out with the disappearances."

"A lot did," Katie said, "but I started looking for

answers after the disappearances because none of them made sense. Aliens, terrorist attacks, none of it. I mean, maybe if only people in America had been affected, but that wasn't the case. Anyway, while I was looking, I came across this website called TruthSeekers. Evidently, others were searching for answers too, and the people who run TruthSeekers claim the disappearances were the rapture that is talked about in the Bible. They post videos every week, a preacher's sermon along with a woman sharing her thoughts about what's happening in the world today. After watching a few of them, I started attending. The church is small, nowhere near the size it used to be, but evidently similar churches have started popping up again all across the world."

Lily wasn't sure which piece of news shocked her more, the fact that churches existed and she hadn't known or the fact that Katie had been attending without telling her. "I'm sorry, did you say you were going to church? Why didn't you tell me?"

Katie sighed. "People who spoke out about the rapture were vilified, and I wasn't sure I believed it. I wanted to go a few times to see what it was all about before I told anyone or asked anyone to go with me. Then these lock-downs happened, and the church was closed anyway, but the website put out a message about a meeting coming up. I think I might go."

"Why?" Lily asked. It had been a long time since she'd

been to church and she wasn't sure how it played into any of this.

"I don't know," Katie said with a shrug. "I just know I felt better when I was there, and who knows, maybe they'll have answers for this too."

Lily tilted her head as she considered her friend. Katie was definitely prone to crazy ideas more than Lily was, but she seemed serious about this. Serious enough that Lily found her curiosity piqued. "Okay, I'll go with you."

The image of Daman Caturix smiling on the TV sent a shiver down Gabe Cross's spine though he had no idea why. He didn't even know who the man was though that was something he was going to remedy right now. He stood and crossed his small living room to grab his laptop. Then he settled back on the couch and began his search.

Daman Caturix was in fact a wealthy billionaire, one who had generally stayed out of sight except for his philanthropic work in delivering vaccines to poor countries. Vaccines? Suddenly, Gabe's stomach churned as if he'd just eaten a piece of moldy cheese. Was that what this was about?

He clicked into the patent registry and searched for Daman Caturix's name. Nothing, but there was some link.

He was sure of it. He brought up a new search and looked for any companies that Caturix owned or was associated with. The list was long, and he was about to bookmark it to return to later when a name caught his eye. Natas Corporation.

Gabe had gone through a period in high school when he'd been into death metal and tried a few drugs. It was not an experience he liked thinking about, but the name of the corporation triggered a memory in his mind. It had been his senior year and he'd been high on dope and out of his mind. He couldn't even remember who the band had been, but he remembered very clearly the chant of Natas ringing out around him as the lead singer urged it on. It was after he sobered up and met Melinda that the significance of that day became clear. Natas - the word that he and others had been chanting was Satan spelled backwards.

Gabe clicked back to the patent registry and entered Natas in the search bar. After a moment, a box appeared on the screen. Patent pending it read, but it was not those two words that sent the hairs on Gabe's neck standing at attention. No, it was the number assigned to the patent that sent ice flooding his veins. 060606. Six, six, six - the mark of the beast. He may not have believed all of what Melinda had told him, but he had been listening. Enough to know that the mark of the beast was bad. Very bad.

Now, he just needed to figure out what to do with the information and who to tell.

He moved his cursor to the X to close the window, but as he did, a message popped up on his screen.

Are you searching for the truth?

He glanced around, looking for a hidden camera or someone to step out of the shadows, but it was just him in the house.

He placed his fingers on the keyboard, unsure of what he was going to type before it appeared on the screen. *Yes.* It was just one word, but Gabe found himself holding his breath as he waited for a response.

Visit TruthSeekers. They can help.

TruthSeekers? What was that? Gabe clicked in the box to type his question, but as he did, the box disappeared. He yanked his fingers from the keyboard and stared at the computer for a moment, waiting for whatever else might come, but the computer did nothing and the single horizontal line continued to blink, waiting for his instructions.

What did he do now?

10

"Finally, it looks like we might be able to get back to some semblance of normal."

"Huh?" Raven pulled her attention from the message on her screen to look up at Jason. He was a few feet away in her easy chair watching the latest press release from Governor Smythe.

"The governor finally agreed to open the counties who are seeing fewer cases. That means us. It means working out with a mask on and taking the temperature of every person who walks in the door, but it's better than nothing. I wonder if Brian knows yet." He pulled out his phone and began tapping on the screen.

"Yeah, that's great," Raven said, and she was happy. Mostly. She was getting tired of take-out food and actually getting to sit down in a restaurant again held appeal if only because she'd been denied the opportunity for so long. However, she wondered how that information fit with the information on her screen.

"It is great, but you don't sound excited," Jason said, coming to sit next to her on the couch. "Why don't you seem excited?"

"I just received this in the TruthSeeker account." Raven had started the webpage shortly after meeting Pastor Ben. It had been the quickest way she knew to start spreading the word of the rapture, and though she'd met few of the people who visited the site, she'd exchanged emails with many of them. This one, however, was new. "The first part is a letter from a virologist, Gabe Cross, who says he has proof that the virus was man-made. He says he'll be making a public statement soon."

"Man-made? So, like it was planned?"

"Yeah," Raven said. "So maybe Kat wasn't so crazy after all, but there's more. He included a few links in his email. The first link is to the patent registry. You know how Daman Caturix has been in the news lately?"

"Yeah, the guy is funding the vaccine companies so we can get back to normal sooner. So what?"

"Well, that guy owns a company called Natas Corporation."

Jason stared at her as if she'd lost her mind. "Okay, and? A lot of people own companies, Raven, and considering the man's a billionaire, I'm sure he owns many companies."

"I'm sure he does own many companies, Jason, but Natas is Satan backwards."

Immediately, she could see his walls going up again. "Raven, we've been through this."

She held up her finger to stop him. "There's more, Jason. Natas Corporation took out a patent on a way to disburse the vaccine. The patent number is 060606." She stared at him, as if waiting for the light bulb to go off in his head.

"Okay, so what?" He was clearly not following the trail she was making for him.

"Zero six, zero six, zero six, Jason, like six, six, six - the mark of the beast." She emphasized the last four words so their impact would not be wasted on him.

"Okay, that is a little creepy," he conceded, "but maybe it was just the next number in line. Do you even know how patent numbers work? Because I don't."

She rolled her eyes at him. Sometimes he was so dense. "I don't know how patent numbers are assigned though I can't imagine a system that would start with zeros at the beginning, but regardless, I'm pretty sure that's not the case, especially with the other link that the message contained." She clicked an open tab and a picture of some strange chart filled the screen.

Jason leaned closer and squinted as he tried to figure out exactly what it said. "What is that?"

"It's the name of Natas Corp's vaccine delivery system. Look, he named it the Human Implantable Quantum Dot Microneedle Vaccination Delivery System."

Jason shrugged. "So, he likes long names. I still don't see the connection, Raven."

"Someone assigned the number of the alphabet to each letter in the words. For example, A is the first letter, so it gets the number one. Every A is one. B is two and so on. Do you understand?"

"I understand that someone has too much time on their hands, but yes, I get it. So what?"

Raven sighed. "So, when you add the numbers up, they equal six-six-six."

The slight teasing grin on Jason's face slid off as he leaned closer to the screen. She watched his eyes track back and forth as they read over the same information she just had. Someone had spelled out the super long name down the side, then assigned the number to each letter. At the bottom, they showed it added up to six-six-six. It was that picture that filled her screen now.

"Okay, that is definitely weird, but it could still be a coincidence."

A coincidence? Jason had been there the day of the disappearances. He'd gone with her to Kat's house and read the letter with her. He'd listened to her tell him what the Bible said was coming. How could he still find any of this a coincidence?

"That would be two huge coincidences, Jason. How many coincidences does it take before it's no longer possible to be a coincidence?"

He ran his hand down his cheek, scratching at his beard. "What even is this quantum dot delivery system? Don't they inject vaccines with a shot or a mist up the nose? I always got vaccines by injection in the Army, but I heard they can do nasal ones now."

"Well, that's where it gets weirder. It's a way to get the vaccine to people, so they can administer it themselves. Evidently, they attach it to something like a Band-Aid with this system, and then people can just put the patch on themselves and the vaccine is administered through the microneedles that pierce your skin."

Jason shook his head and scooted back a little on the couch. "Nuh uh, that sounds weird and little too futuristic to me. I don't like shots, but I'll take mine the old-fashioned way."

"Wait, there's more. Evidently his system needs some other substance to make it adhere correctly, and the substance he chose is this binding agent called Luciferase."

This time Jason's eyebrows lifted and his eyes widened at her. "Luciferase? As in Lucifer?"

"Still think it's a coincidence?" Raven asked.

"Luciferase is actually a luminescent, so it's named after that, but interesting, don't you think? Anyway, this Luciferase makes it light up in your body under a blacklight."

"So, people could check to see if you've received the vaccine?"

Finally, it seemed the pieces were falling into place for Jason. "Exactly, and what would be the purpose to knowing if people have had the vaccine?"

"To keep them from entering places and spreading the virus, but if that's the case, why even open up now? I mean it's limited, but if the plan is to make people want this vaccine, why open at all?"

Raven shrugged. "I don't know. Maybe to give people a little hope before they take it away again. Whatever the reason, I have a feeling this might be the mark of the beast mentioned in the Bible."

"Wait, wait, wait," he said, waving his hands. "Why would they use the vaccine to be the mark? Didn't you say it was about pledging loyalty to the Antichrist?"

"I always thought it was an actual pledging of loyalty, but what if it's hidden in this? Think about it. We were told masks didn't work, then we were told they were the only way to stop the spread. Even with them, things aren't going back to normal - not the normal we want anyway. There's already been one story of a man getting killed over not wearing a mask." Raven was fairly certain there were more stories out there like that or would be soon.

"Now they're beginning to tell us that vaccines are the only way to get back to normal. If they can now see who's had a vaccine and who hasn't, why wouldn't they use that as an excuse to keep people from shopping or attending events? They could easily tell us we are endangering people's health without one and can't enter until we have one."

"Okay, let's say I'm buying all this," Jason said slowly. "What would be the point of restricting people who don't get the vaccine?"

"What's the point of the lockdowns and the mask mandate now?" Raven asked. "Control. It's all about control. We've all been following the rules because we believed them, because we thought it would make us safer and help us return to normal, but what if this has all been a test to see how much they can control us? Those who don't wear masks can't return to work. Some businesses are even kicking customers out who don't have them or refusing them service. It's quickly becoming more of a law than a mandate. What happens if a vaccine becomes mandatory? And what if it's this vaccine?"

"Then we don't take the vaccine," Jason said as if it was the simplest thing in the world. "We're both young and healthy anyway, so there's no need. My bartending job might require it, but Brian never will, and you can work anywhere with your skills."

Raven sighed. He still didn't see the bigger picture, but it was a start. If she could at least keep him from getting the vaccine, maybe she could save him until she could convince him that all of this was predicted and that the only real solution was God.

11

Gabe Cross stared at the small house and checked the address again. Raven Rader, the mind behind the TruthSeekers website, had said they couldn't meet in the regular church due to the governor's orders, and this was the address she had given him, but he still wasn't sure he was in the right place. However, maybe his apprehension had more to do with the fact that his life was spinning out of control for the second time in less than a year than the fact that he was meeting a woman for the first time that he'd only spoken to over the computer up until now.

After his research into Daman Caturix, he'd realized he could no longer remain quiet about what he knew. He'd called a press conference, shared his findings, and been fired shortly thereafter as he'd been nearly certain he would be. Not only that, but he'd been ostracized by his fellow scientists. Still, he wasn't sorry he'd done it. Though he did not know the man, everything he'd found pointed to Daman Caturix being evil, and while he hadn't mentioned the man's name on the air, he'd said enough about the virus being man-made to get him blacklisted from every scientific community. Well, the scientific communities that were allowed to speak. He was beginning to find more brave souls like himself speaking the truth through videos on the internet. However, they were being taken down nearly as fast as they went up. The social media sites had declared war on anyone who spoke against the accepted narrative by either removing their content or shutting down their account entirely.

Thankfully, he'd spoken with Raven before going on camera, and she'd promised that whatever happened, he had a home with them. If he was right, they'd all be going into hiding sooner or later anyway. He was just speeding his time frame up, but hopefully, he would change a few minds and save a few souls on his way.

He knocked three times on the door, pausing before the last rap as Raven had stated he should. There was probably little need for the secrecy right now, but it would come in handy soon.

The door opened, and he found himself staring at an edgy woman with long dark hair. A small silver ring glistened in one nostril. Had he met her on the street, he might have given her a wide berth, but when she smiled at him, he felt instantly at ease.

"You must be Gabe," she said, opening the door wider. "Come in, we've been waiting for you."

He wondered who "we" was, but as he stepped into the living room, he could see a group of about ten people staring back at him.

"This isn't everybody, of course. Due to the governor's orders, we had to start meeting in smaller groups and communicating by phone and secure video channels, but this is everyone local. I'm Raven, as you probably figured out, and this is Jason." She pointed to a tall, muscular man with a beard but a bald head. "He's not quite a believer yet, but he is against government control. Plus, I've known him the longest, and I vouch for his trustworthiness.

"Next to him are Brian and his wife Dani." She walked over to an older looking man with salt and pepper hair and a blonde woman who looked like she could bench press anyone in the room. "Brian owns the kickboxing gym where Jason works, and Dani worked as a nurses' assistant until she was laid off due to the virus."

Gabe smiled and nodded, but he knew he would not remember everyone's name tonight. "Next, we have Lily and Katie. Lily also attends the gym. She and Katie will be Seniors in high school next year."

"If we ever get to go back," the blonde one he assumed was Lily said.

"Right. If." Raven moved on to an older man in a button-down shirt and pants. "This is Pastor Benjamin Westley. He's been our guide through all of this so far, helping us make sense of the book of Revelation."

"Well, as much sense as we can," the pastor said, "and you can call me Ben."

"And finally, we have Nathan. He was in charge of the sound system at Mountain Home before the rapture. We haven't had much need for that as we've been pretty small, but he helps with our communications."

"It's nice to meet you all." Gabe looked around the room and then back to Raven. "Wait, didn't you say there was another doctor too?"

Raven nodded. "Yes, Dr. Candace Markham. Unfortunately, she lives up in Seattle right now and is an ER doc, so she's on the front lines of NCAV. We keep in touch, but she hasn't been able to come down in a few weeks. However, I'm sure she'll be joining us as soon as the vaccine begins rolling out."

Raven motioned for Gabe to take one of the empty seats before taking one herself. "Everyone, this is Gabe Cross, the brave virologist who came forward to share with the world that NCAV was indeed man-made and not transmitted by bat or at a market like the media has been claiming."

"No offense, but how exactly do you know that?" Jason asked.

"Every virus has markers," Gabe said, adjusting his position to lean forward slightly. "Natural viruses differ slightly from each other, but they differ greatly from manufactured viruses. Natural viruses appear round with short stubby knobs under a microscope. Manufactured viruses have nodules that are much longer and thinner. The NCAV virus is definitely the latter."

"In addition to Dr. Cross's findings on the virus is what he found out about Daman Caturix which I've already shared with all of you," Raven said. "Now, we still don't know exactly what the play is here. As Jason said to me the other day, why open up just to close down again? I don't have those answers, but what Pastor Ben and I do agree on is that this is the beginning.

"We believe the virus was put into play to create fear and to condition the people to do whatever the government said. We're already seeing that with our young and healthy friends who face little risk of death with this virus but refuse to get together or go back to work. We see it with the people berating and attacking those who refuse to wear masks, and I'm afraid it will only get worse. My guess is that this vaccine Caturix is backing will be fast tracked out to the public as a means of "getting back to normal." Even though most of us in this room are not at risk, we will be asked to take the vaccine for those who are. That request will soon turn into a demand and then into a threat that will keep us from being able to enter stores, purchase items, et cetera."

"What happens then?" the other younger girl asked, fear threading her voice.

"We need to start preparing before then," Ben said. "There is plenty of room at the church where we can store supplies for now. When you go to the store, pick up a few extra canned goods or boxed items - anything that will keep for a time. Bring them to the church and Nathan and I will store them. Nathan is also working on building a secret door where we will be able to enter the supply room and retrieve the supplies should they ever bar us from the church."

Raven nodded as Ben finished and gestured to the space around them. "This house belonged to Kat, who was raptured. It hasn't been used for a while, and I don't think it will be on their radar for a while either, so anyone who needs a place to stay is welcome here. I'll get a keycode lock installed so we don't need keys. I've also got someone looking for a larger safehouse for us. We're spread out over Washington right now, but when the time comes, we will be safer together."

She turned to Gabe. "I'm hoping that perhaps you can work on a safe vaccine for us. While most of us aren't at risk, we do have some elderly members who are. Plus, I have no idea if they'll find a way to mutate the virus."

Gabe nodded. He'd been thinking the exact same

thing after speaking with Raven the first time. "I'm just one man and vaccines like this generally take years, but if I can get my hands on a dose, I may be able to isolate the part that works while eliminating the Luciferase."

"Okay, we'll add that to the list. I'll send a message out to the other groups and let them know the plan. I know this all sounds scary, but I do believe we're in the eye of the storm right now. I believe things will appear to get better before they get worse. Please keep your eyes open for anything out of the ordinary, and whatever you do, don't take the vaccine."

12

TWO MONTHS LATER

Conflicting feelings coursed through Lily as she turned off the alarm. The last few months had almost felt normal, minus the limit on gatherings and the wearing of masks. In fact, they'd been so close to normal that she was returning to school today. Most of the schools in Washington were starting the year the way they'd ended - remotely - but Lily's school was smaller and because of that, the school had decided it could return to in-person learning and still follow the Governor's requirements. It was those requirements that made Lily's blood boil though.

First and foremost, masks were required at school every day. Lily had purchased several different varieties in hopes that something would be comfortable enough to wear all day long, but she had never worn a mask longer than it took to run errands in town. What if she couldn't breathe? What if it caused her to break out or pass out? That hadn't happened so far, but she'd read about mask acne online, and it sounded gross and unsanitary.

Second, they were going to have to stay six feet from each other during classes and lunch. Conversations weren't impossible to carry on with that much distance, but they were much harder to keep quiet. Everyone would be able to hear what everyone else was discussing. At a high school in general that was a bad thing, but with Lily and Katie probably having a much different opinion than their classmates on the vaccine that was due to be released any day, it took on a whole new meaning.

Third, there were new requirements about having to get their temperature taken every day and answering questions about symptoms. Brian had been forced to implement the same procedure at the gym, but after two months of no one presenting with a fever, he'd finally stopped doing it. Nor did he require a mask to work out. They had to wear it in and out of the gym, but they were able to take it off to work out. Thank goodness.

The school, unfortunately, wasn't going to be so gracious. They'd sent home a list of the symptoms that could keep a student out of school. It was not a short list, and if they answered yes to even one of them, they had to be home for ten days or get a test to prove they weren't infected with the virus. If the virus had unusual symptoms, like extreme vomiting or a crazy rash, it wouldn't have been that big of a deal, but the symptoms for this virus were largely the same for a cold or the flu - runny nose, cough, fever, and congestion.

That meant at some point this year, Lily would probably have to be out and learning from home because it never failed that she got a cold at least once a year. In fact, she was surprised that she hadn't gotten sick just from the paranoia that was running rampant through her state. Add to that the stress that school could close literally at any time, and Lily wasn't sure she even wanted to get out of bed.

The principal had made it clear in his welcome letter that the health expert didn't like them being open until the vaccine was available, and the woman would probably be watching Lily's, and the few other small schools who were opening, like a hawk just waiting for some random case or broken rule so she could sweep in and slam the doors shut once again. Lily had no idea why the state seemed intent on keeping kids out of school, especially since students made up fewer than one percent of the NCAV cases worldwide, but she figured it was part of the scare tactic as well.

Kicking back the covers, she sighed and rolled out of bed. After a quick shower, she stood, staring at the clothes in her closet. This time last year, she had been so excited to return to school that she had laid out her clothes the night before, but this year the excitement wasn't the same. Even though she was getting to go back, she knew it wouldn't be the same, and the threat of having to return to distance learning was never far from her mind. Grabbing a pair of jeans and her black long-sleeved shirt with a silver heart on it, she pulled them on and headed downstairs.

The aroma of freshly brewed coffee along with the tempting scent of bacon and eggs greeted her as she made her way toward the kitchen. At least her mother had more time to make breakfast since her job was still requiring her to work from home.

"Hey, sweetie," she said, glancing up with a smile. "You ready for school today?"

Lily shrugged and grabbed a mug from the cabinet. After filling it up, she decided she could finagle bacon and eggs into her diet today. After all, Bryce wouldn't be at school this year, having graduated last year. There wasn't really anyone else she was trying to impress.

"Yeah, I guess," Lily said with a sigh as she sat down and filled her plate. "Though I'm not looking forward to wearing a mask all day."

Her mother flashed a sympathetic smile and patted her hand. "I know, but I bet it won't be as bad as you think. At least you get to be back in school with your friends instead of stuck home here with me."

There was that silver lining. Lily loved her mother,

and it wasn't being stuck home with her that drove Lily crazy, it was just being stuck at home. Her gym had opened, but most places were still closed. There was no place to go for entertainment - no movie theaters, no bowling alleys, even the outdoor go-cart place was still closed.

Before Lily could say anything more, the alarm on her phone went off. With a sigh, she stuffed a final bite of eggs in her mouth before wrapping the bacon in a paper towel. It, at least, could travel.

"Do you have everything you need?" her mother asked as she stood and gathered her bag.

"Yep, I packed my masks and supplies last night." Lily opened the fridge and pulled out the brown bag she had put together the night before. "Along with my lunch." She and Katie didn't usually eat lunch at the school, but that was another new restriction - no leaving campus due to the temperature checks that had to be performed every morning. Just another thing in the long list of things about this year that sucked.

A surreal feeling blanketed Lily as she pulled into the parking lot at school. Nothing looked that different minus a few small signs pointing to the areas where students would need to check in and get their temperatures checked, but the mood felt off. Almost dark. Lily looked around as she climbed out of the car, but nothing jumped out at her. There was no dark stranger waiting to attack her, so why did she have goosebumps erupting on her arms?

Maybe it was because there was no Katie. She almost always arrived before Lily did, so, where was she?

Suddenly, Lily wondered if she had come on the wrong day. The school had decided to do what they called a "slow start" in order to limit the number of students in the building for the first few days. The freshmen and sophomores had been first, but Lily was fairly certain they had come yesterday. Juniors and Seniors were today. Weren't they?

Deciding that Katie was either late or waiting inside, Lily hoisted her backpack over her shoulder, put the breath-impeding contraption over her face, and headed for the main door of the building.

During a normal year, there were three entrances to her high school open, but due to the new regulations, only one door was unlocked, and two staff members manned it, both wearing masks and holding clipboards. One, she recognized as Mrs. Fox, but the other was a new face.

"Good morning, Lily," Mrs. Fox said. Though Lily couldn't see the kind woman's smile, she could hear it in her voice, which provided a small modicum of comfort. "How was your summer?"

Lily snorted and shook her head. "Lame. How about yours?"

Her hazel eyes twinkled behind her mask. "The same,

but I'm glad to be here at least." She turned the clipboard toward Lily, so she could read it. "Do you or anyone in your household have any of these symptoms?"

Lily scanned the long list - cough, cold, congestion, fever, vomiting, loss of smell, fatigue, runny nose, body aches, and known exposure to anyone who had the virus. It sounded like the side effects listed in one of those terrible TV ads. She shook her head again, both in answer to the question and at the sheer craziness involved in that list.

"Okay, let me get your temperature." Mrs. Fox held an infrared thermometer close to Lily's forehead for a moment before waving her through the door. "You're all good. Have a great day."

Hah. A great day breathing in her own expelled air all day? Somehow, she doubted that. Already, she felt hot and itchy though how much of that was due to the mask itself or just her pure hatred of them, she didn't know.

A sigh spilled from her lips as she stepped inside and saw the arrows of blue tape pointing out the direction of recommended traffic. The grocery stores had done this too though no one appeared able to follow it. Lily doubted students would be any better.

Continuing to her locker, she shoved her bag in and pulled out her schedule. The school had allowed students to come in small numbers a few days prior to pick up their schedules. Lily had science first, just like last year, followed by English, choir, math, Spanish, history, and creative writing. Not a super stressful load, but heavy enough. She grabbed her science folder and glanced around again for Katie. Where was that girl?

The halls were eerily silent; only a few other people could be spotted and none were close to her. Instinctively, Lily knew this mainly had to do with the fact that they were on a split schedule and half of the students weren't here, but it was still creepy. Shutting her locker door, she glanced around again for Katie, but she was still nowhere to be seen. It felt strange walking to class without her. Lily couldn't remember a time they hadn't walked to class together.

Mr. Higgins was at the white board scrawling the day's objectives across it when she entered. "Good morning, Lily," he said with barely a glance in her direction. She supposed when a teacher had a student for two years, they started to learn the unique sound each student made.

"Hey, Mr. Higgins." Lily grabbed her usual seat and dropped her purse beside her. Though she knew touching her mask was frowned upon, she could not keep her fingers from gravitating to the restrictive barrier and pulling it from her face slightly. Her breath burned against her nose and mouth like a sunburn the day after. "Do you think we'll have to wear masks the whole year?"

Mr. Higgins was not only the science teacher, but he had studied diseases in college. He'd also been pretty vocal about the shutdown at the end of last school year being unnecessary, so Lily trusted his opinion.

With a sigh, he turned from the board and met her gaze. "I don't know, Lily. I'm wearing this mask because the school says we have to, and they're saying we have to because the governor says we have to, but I personally don't believe it does much to protect us, especially since so many people wear it wrong or touch it all day. Sometimes though, we have to follow the rules even when they don't make much sense to us."

"For how long though?" The words spilled out of her mouth before she could stop them, and they emerged harsher than she meant for them to. Pausing to take a deep breath and swallow some of her frustration, she tried again, softening her tone. "I just mean, is there a point where we become like sheep following the wrong things?"

His eyes remained on hers and though she could not see his lips, she was sure he was smiling. But not the patronizing type of smile, a genuine one that meant he was proud of her. "I do think there is a point where it could become like that, and I honestly hope we don't get to that point. However, I don't think we are there yet. Let's follow the rules for now and see how things go."

Lily wanted to ask what his thoughts were on the impending vaccine, but before she could, more students began filing in. Though she recognized most of them, there were a few she could not place. Whether that was because they were new or because they had changed so much over the summer that they were unrecognizable behind their mask, Lily wasn't sure.

Katie slid into the room seconds before the bell rang. A look of frustration creased her forehead, and for the first time in a long time, she had no coffee. Something was clearly wrong. People might not be able to sit in a coffee joint, but the drive thrus had been open for a while now.

"Are you okay?" Lily whispered as Katie took the desk nearest hers. Even the desks were placed six feet apart, so Lily couldn't be as quiet as she would have liked, but Katie heard. Her lips pursed together, and she shook her head.

"I'll tell you later."

Mr. Higgins began class then, but Lily found it hard to focus on what he was saying. Not only was the hot air she kept exhaling and re-breathing in constantly on her mind, but a stubborn itchy sensation had taken up residence on her face. Her forehead, her cheeks, her nose - everything pulsed with a desire to be scratched and refraining from it appeared futile. Her fingers twitched on the desk as she fought the urge.

When the bell finally rang signaling the end of first period, Lily gathered up her things and realized she had missed most of the class. Thankfully it was the first day of school and there was generally less work assigned, but this was Mr. Higgins' class, and he seemed to never care whether it was September or April when it came to assigning work.

"What happened?" Lily asked Katie as they joined the throng of students filling the hallway. The blue arrows that lined the floor were largely ignored, and students, having not seen their friends in months, conveniently forgot (or ignored) the social distance rule as they high-fived or hugged in the hallway. Yeah, this was going to work so well.

"I was halfway here when I forgot my stupid mask and had to turn around and go home." Annoyance filled Katie's voice, but Lily had a hard time believing all of it stemmed from forgetting her mask.

"First of all, I'm sure they have some here you could have borrowed. I doubt you'll be the only one to forget your mask at some point this year, but why didn't you just leave it in your bag or in your car like I do?"

"It does no good hanging in your car," Katie said, throwing her hands up.

"It does no good anyway," Lily said. Hadn't Katie been attending the same meetings with Raven and the others that she had? Why was she acting like suddenly she believed all the hype? "This is all about control. Remember?"

Suddenly Katie's demeanor shifted. Her eyes flashed around, and her fingers darted out, grabbing Lily's arm and squeezing. "You can't say stuff like that out loud. Who knows who might be listening?"

"Listening?" Now Lily was starting to worry. Katie was acting weirder than normal. "Who's going to be listening?"

Katie shook her head, but there was definitely something going on with her. And more than the fact that she'd had to return home to get a mask. Lily was determined to find out what, but the warning bell sounded before she could press the issue, and the girls dashed for their separate classrooms.

The rest of the morning flew by and dragged at the same time. The routine of being back in the classroom made the time go by quicker than it had at home, but the constant heat against Lily's lips and the pressure on the back of her ears from the straps of the mask served as a constant reminder of how much of the day remained.

When lunch finally arrived, Lily walked into the gym which no longer served as a gym but the makeshift cafeteria since it was bigger. It felt weird calling it a cafeteria though since the school wasn't even serving food. Brown bags or nothing. That seemed to be the mantra of the year. Only two choices - one bad and the other worse.

With a sigh, Lily sank down onto one of the seats. Last year, the tables had teemed with students laughing and leaning over each other to share a video or a funny meme on each other's phones. Now, there were giant stickers on the seats students could actually sit on, and the large tables were limited to three students so they could be socially distant while they ate. New slender tables that only allowed a student at each end had also been added, but as Lily knew a quiet conversation would be impossible at one of those, she had opted for the former.

The only redeeming grace was that lunch meant food and food meant having an unimpeded access to the mouth which meant no mask. Lily ripped hers off and inhaled the fresh air. As she watched the students around her do the same, she realized again how silly and futile this all was. Students were forced to wear a mask during every class, but here in the lunchroom, they could all have them off. If the virus was really airborne as the media claimed, wouldn't the students all just get infected here? Where had common sense gone?

Katie arrived a moment later and set her own mask on the table before opening her lunch.

"You want to tell me what's really going on?" Lily asked.

Katie sighed as she pulled a sandwich from a ziplock bag. "It's my parents. They want me to get the vaccine."

"What?" Lily realized she had said the word louder than she meant to when heads turned her direction. She lowered her voice and hissed, "Katie, you can't."

"I know, but they're my parents. What am I supposed to do?"

"Have you told them about Caturix and the patent?"

Katie bit her lip and shook her head. "No, you know how they are. They believe everything the media is saying. They didn't even want me to return to school this year, but I refused to spend another year at home on a laptop."

Katie's mother worked for the state, and they had declared their workers wouldn't be returning any time soon. Her father managed one of the local grocery stores, and while he hadn't been forced to close like other businesses had, he was paranoid about contracting the virus. He wore gloves all day at work, changing them every time he went to the bathroom or consciously touched his face. Lily had also been surprised they'd let Katie return to school.

"I can't blame you there, but don't worry, we'll figure something out. The vaccine isn't even here yet, and I bet even when it is released, we won't be the first in line to get it."

"I hope not, but anyway, that's what made me late today, and it's kind of thrown my whole day off."

"Well, at least today is almost over. You can come over tonight and we'll celebrate the first day of school with ice cream. How's that?"

Katie's lips pulled into a slight smile, but the light did not reach her eyes. It might take more than ice cream to bring her bubbly friend back, but Lily wasn't going to give up.

"When you girls are done, please remember to put your masks back on."

Lily looked up at the woman speaking to them. Her voice was unfamiliar, and though she could only see the woman's eyes and forehead over her mask, her face did not seem familiar either. Her eyes were the color of coal, and though Lily would not have thought it possible, her hair appeared a shade darker. Her skin, though not abnormally pale, seemed that way in contrast to her eyes and hair.

"I'm sorry, who are you?" Lily asked, trying not to sound as annoyed as she felt.

The woman's eyes crinkled, and Lily knew a patronizing smile lay under her mask. "My name is Ms. Chemosh, but you can call me Ms. C. I'm the new counselor here."

A counselor? This was news to Lily. Their school was so small that the teachers and office staff had served as make-shift counselors. Why did they have one this year? "What does a counselor do in a school this small?"

"More than you'd expect." Her tone dripped like honey, but it did not sound sweet in Lily's ear. Instead, it sounded grating like squealing brakes. "I help students figure out their graduation plan and apply to colleges. I also moderate issues between students, and of course, this year, I'm happy to help with any student feeling anxious about the virus."

"Oh, that's good to know," Katie said, but Lily could tell she was simply placating the woman. "We'll be sure to put our masks back on when we're done eating."

"Very well," Ms. C said. Her eyes lingered a moment longer on them before she turned and headed off to another table.

Lily rolled her eyes as the woman walked away to share the reminder with another table. She didn't have enough knowledge of this woman to form a solid opinion yet, but this whole nonsense of wearing a mask as soon as they finished eating was silly. By the time they finished eating, they would have spent at least twenty minutes with their masks off. If the virus were truly in the air, they would all have been exposed and putting a mask on after that certainly wasn't going to save them. Besides the majority of the evidence still pointed to the fact that kids rarely got the virus and when they did, their cases were mild.

"I'll see you after school?" Lily asked Katie as they stood and headed toward the trash cans. They didn't have any of their afternoon classes together.

"Yep, see you then."

13

"This makes no sense."

Gabe looked over to see Raven staring at the numbers on her screen and shaking her head. "What's the matter?" he asked, crossing to her side.

"Something isn't adding up. Smythe passed the mask mandate months ago, right?"

"Yeah, as did many states. Why?"

"Well, you and I both know that masks are pretty useless, but even with them being useless, it doesn't explain why positive cases are still occurring at such a high rate. Deaths seem to be lower which makes sense as we know so much more about how to treat this now, but why, if we are all masking and socially distancing, are cases still going up?"

"Well, the virus is highly contagious." Gabe pulled up a chair beside her.

"I know, but something still feels off. Plus, look at this." She clicked a different tab, and an email popped up on the screen. "Check this out." She clicked on a picture inside the email, enlarging it before turning the screen toward Gabe.

He leaned closer to study the picture. "Okay, that looks like a hospital, but it appears empty."

"It is," Raven said. "Candace sent me this today. She said hospitalizations from NCAV are fewer than ten people most weeks, but no one is allowed to say anything. They were threatened with termination if they leaked any pictures."

Gabe scratched at his chin. "So, there's a rise in positive cases but a decrease in hospitalizations and deaths, but the government clearly does not want us to see that. Why?"

From behind them, an alert sounded on the TV proclaiming breaking news. They turned from the computer to watch.

"We are pleased to announce that the first NCAV vaccine, sponsored by Daman Caturix, has passed quality control checks and Dr. Goodman will be receiving the very first dose," the news anchor said with a smile that was meant to be consoling but had the opposite effect on Gabe.

There was still so much he didn't know, didn't understand, about how they planned to put the mark of the beast in the vaccine. The time crunch pressed down on him, an invisible weighted blanket that held no comfort at all.

"They are televising him getting vaccinated?" Raven asked, leaning forward in her chair. "This has got to be a part of it, Gabe, getting the masses to want this. I can't remember a time they've ever televised a vaccination before. Have you?"

He bit the inside of his lip as he mentally reviewed the information again. An increase in cases but lower deaths and hospitalizations that were being hidden. A rushed vaccine that could be associated with the mark of the beast. A televised vaccination to portray the message that the vaccine was safe. He had to find out what was in the vaccine.

"No, I haven't either," he said, answering her question, "but I still have nothing, Raven. Nothing that tells me how they're putting the mark in the vaccine, how to replicate it, nothing." He wasn't used to feeling like he had no control, and he didn't like it.

"It's okay. We'll figure something out. It will take some time to get it to the people on the front lines who want it before they start mandating it."

"Yeah, but what about Candace? She'll be one of the first pressured to take it, won't she?" Gabe had yet to meet the beloved doctor, but she was forefront on his mind in all of this.

"Candace has the same information that we do. She may not have been able to make it down lately, but we've been emailing. She's prepared to quit if she has to when the time comes. Until then, let's just pray we figure something out."

Raven had yet to look away from the television, and Gabe couldn't help feeling as though she did not understand the gravity of the situation.

"Wait, he's not the only one getting a vaccine?" Raven's voice held a note of disbelief as well as something like awe.

Gabe turned his full attention to the television. She was right. Lined up behind Dr. Goodman were several prominent members of congress as well as a few other doctors who had been spouting the same nonsense Dr. Goodman had.

"Some of those people aren't even in the high-risk category," Gabe said softly. "Why are they getting a vaccine first?"

He rose from the desk and moved to the couch to get a closer look at the television. Something about this had his bones buzzing. Why would they be vaccinating people on camera? Sure, he knew there were those in the world who believed vaccines were more harmful than helpful, but could there be that many?

"How do you feel, Dr. Goodman?" the doctor giving the dose asked as soon as the shot was removed from Goodman's arm. Wait, shot? Weren't they supposed to be using the human application system he had researched? Had that been a ruse? A ploy to throw them off track?

"They're using a needle," Raven said as she sat down beside him as if catching his mental thoughts.

"Yeah, why? Does that mean they aren't using Lucerifase?"

From the corner of his eye, he could see Raven shake her head, but like himself, her eyes were still glued to the screen.

"Dr. Goodman?" the doctor asked again.

"Huh, I'm sorry, what did you say?" Dr. Goodman asked.

"I asked how you feel, sir?"

"Feel? I feel... amazing. Almost as if I can feel the vaccine working."

Gabe had never been a big fan of Dr. Goodman who had always seemed like he cared more about publicity than health in Gabe's opinion, but this reaction was weird. The hairs on the back of his neck joined his bones in voicing their apprehension.

The doctor administering the vaccine stared at Dr. Goodman for a moment before he was heard whispering, "You're done. You can go now, Dr. Goodman."

"Go? Yes, of course. Thank you for your service, and

thank you Daman Caturix for the financial backing that made this day possible." The smile that split Goodman's face as he stood reminded Gabe of Jack Nicolson in The Shining. On the outside, there was nothing wrong with it, but on the inside? Well, he didn't know what was wrong with it, but something definitely was.

Dr. Goodman moved off stage, but Gabe watched his demeanor as he did. He would have to find old footage of Goodman to be sure, but he had a hunch that this time had been much stiffer, more mechanical. Why?

The next patron, a senator from New York took the spotlight. Once again, the doctor prepared the syringe and then stuck her arm. Gabe didn't focus there though. He kept his eyes glued on the woman's face, and when he saw it, he shivered.

"Hand me the remote," he said to Raven, still not taking his eyes off the screen. He had to be sure.

"Why? What did you see?"

"Nothing good," he said as she placed the remote in his hand. He backed up the screen and then pushed the button to make it play forward screen by screen. "There! Did you see that?" he asked when it crossed the screen again.

"Her eyes."

Gabe knew from the fear in Raven's voice that she had seen the same thing he had. There was a moment, a single moment after receiving the vaccine that her eyes had rolled back as if she'd passed out or fainted. The next moment, she was staring at the camera again. He punched the rewind button to replay Goodman's scene and was not surprised to see the same reaction.

"What does it mean?" Raven asked.

"I'm not sure," Gabe responded. He had a few guesses, but they were just that - guesses. "I need to get my hands on a dose of that vaccine to be sure, but I think this may not be the mark of the beast. At least not yet."

"Then what is it?"

"The next step to controlling people."

He was reminded of a novel he'd read in high school, the story Fahrenheit 451 by Ray Bradbury. In that book, the government had used seashell radios to inundate people with propaganda they wanted them to believe, to make them behave the way the government wanted. What if, instead of a seashell radio, they had put something in the vaccine? Some invisible element that would alter people's minds, their perceptions? What if this was how they convinced masses to tattoo the numbers 666 on their hands or foreheads and believe it was a good idea?

"Do you think Candace would be able to get me a dose of the vaccine?"

"There's only one way to find out."

14

"You want me to do what?" Candace hissed into the phone. She was locked inside a private bathroom in the hospital where she didn't think anyone would hear her conversation, but she still kept her volume low. There was no telling how much could be heard outside or if anyone had seen her enter.

"I need you to get me a dose of the vaccine," the man on the other end said.

Gabe Cross. At least that's who Raven had said he was. A well-known and well-respected virologist who had recently lost his status after declaring the virus to be man-made and not natural. But Candace had never met him. She had no idea if this man was who he said he was or if he was a spy working for someone else. Now, he was asking her to try and steal a vaccine dosage? One that would draw suspicion when it showed up missing?

"I could lose my job. I know I said that I'd have to stop one day, but I'm helping so many people on the inside here. Not only am I actually treating patients, but I get to talk to them about God and the disappearances as they recover." She sounded like she was making excuses, but she couldn't help it; she did feel like she was helping this way. How could she help if she lost her job and therefore her hospital privileges?

"And that's important, I know, but if I'm right, this is even more important," Gabe said. "I think there is something in that vaccine that is brainwashing people, allowing them to be susceptible to propaganda. You think the denial of true information is bad now, but it will only get worse if I'm right."

Deep down she knew he was right. After all, this wasn't normal life. Everything from here on out had a much deeper purpose, deeper meaning. It probably had all along, but she'd been too busy to see it. Too busy. She paused. Was she falling into the same trap again? Was she putting her security with work over the more important spiritual matter?

"There has to be another way."

There was a pause, but she could hear Gabe's soft breath on the other end of the line. When he spoke, his tone had changed - softer, more serious. "There might be one other way, but it's a huge risk, Candace."

"What is it?" He might be right, but didn't she at least deserve to hear both options and decide for herself?

"You could get the vaccine and then send me some vials of your blood to study."

Well, that sounded much simpler. Why hadn't he suggested that in the first place?

"But that comes with a possible heavy cost," Gabe continued. "If something in this vaccine is altering people's minds, it could happen to you and might cause you to take the mark without even knowing it."

Candace chewed on her lip as she thought about the choice. Did she really want to jeopardize her soul just to work a little longer? Besides, there would probably be people in the TruthSeeker group who would need a doctor. She would be of no help to them if she was brain-washed. "Okay, I'll try to get a vial of the vaccine. If that doesn't work, then I'll take the vaccine and cross my fingers that I'll be okay."

"I know neither of these are great choices, but it's a new world."

Indeed it was, and one that she was no longer sure she liked.

Katie stood on the curb as Lily pulled in, bouncing slightly on her toes. Though not visible, Lily could feel the cloud of nervous energy that buzzed around her as she climbed out of the car and pulled her mask on. She had always enjoyed Katie meeting her in the morning, but now a trickle of irritation ignited in her belly. Not so much at Katie, but at the predicament. The school had stressed the need to wear masks even outside if students were closer than six feet. The walk from her car to the front door was less than a hundred feet, but it was a hundred feet of fresh air before she was forced to stifle her breathing all day. However today, Katie meeting her in the parking lot robbed her of that hundred feet, and even the coffee she offered didn't totally abate Lily's irritation.

"Did you hear?"

They were three innocent words, but when Katie said them, they held the weight of the world, and it seemed like she was saying them a lot this year. Lily shook her head. After Katie had left her house last night, she had curled up with a book and passed out. No news, no internet, no depressing virus stories - she'd had enough of those to last a lifetime.

"So, you know how some of the states in the east and south already opened up?"

Lily nodded. There was a part of her that wished she lived in Florida. They had shut down initially, like the rest of the states, but a few weeks later when they realized the virus mainly affected older people or those with pre-existing conditions, they had opened their economy back up. There had been a spike in cases, but their governor had kept them open, and now they were completely open for business. Schools were in session, sports were occurring, and concerts could even take place. They were even back in their churches.

"Yeah, I wish we were there, but I'm assuming that's not your story."

Katie shook her head as they walked toward the front entrance for their temperature check. "Not at all. There are stories online this morning that students back east were kicked out of school for not wearing masks or following the six-foot distance rule. And," she emphasized the word drawing it out, "our governor just declared that students in dorms have to wear their masks in every place except their own room."

"That is so dumb. Haven't they read the stories about apartments and people getting sick who never even went out?"

A few months ago, just after the pandemic struck the whole of the United States completely, results began trickling in of people in apartments getting the virus even though they'd never left their house. At first, the people in charge had blamed it on food deliveries, claiming that those people must have ordered groceries or meals that were infected by the delivery drivers and then gotten infected when they touched the items to bring them inside.

That was later debunked though, and the only logical conclusion they were left with was that apartment buildings shared heating and cooling vents which meant that if someone in one apartment was sick, their germs were going into the vents and then being pushed out into everyone else's houses. With that logic, it made no sense to require masks in a dorm building but not in a dorm room because students would be exposed to the virus when they went into their rooms, but they couldn't very well mandate that people wear masks in their bedrooms. Lily could barely function all day wearing one; she could not imagine trying to sleep with one on.

"Who knows?" Katie said with a shrug, "but this does not bode well for us. If they are enacting crazy rules like that in states that have opened up more than we have, what does it mean for us?"

A heavy sensation settled in Lily's stomach. Nothing good. That was for sure.

They reached the front door of the school and waited for one of the teachers to open it. Lily sighed as she thought of last year when the doors of the school had been unlocked. Students had been free to enter and leave as they pleased during certain times, but now, the school was more like a prison. Only one entrance was allowed to be used, and they had to be let into it by the people in charge.

The door swung open, and the two girls stepped inside. Mrs. Brinkley, one of the math teachers, was checking temperatures today, but after marking them clear, she handed them a sheet of paper. Lily's eyes scanned the print. A mandatory assembly had been called today - by grade levels of course because, even though the school was small, it was impossible for all the grades to be socially distanced in the gym at one time.

"What do you think this is about?" Lily asked as they continued to their lockers.

"I don't know, but I doubt it's good."

Katie was prone to exaggerations, but this time, Lily wholeheartedly agreed.

The Senior assembly time was right after lunch, and Lily's nerves tightened with each class. Even the short mask break lunch afforded did not entirely calm her nerves. A feeling that something bad was about to be disclosed cloaked her shoulders like an invisible blanket. Katie must have felt the same because for the first time since the two had been friends, she was quiet the entire time.

When the lunch bell rang, the girls tossed their trash

away and then returned to the table. The rest of the Seniors and Juniors filled in around them. A moment later, Mr. Shane, the principal appeared with a microphone in hand.

"Thank you all for staying. This won't be a long assembly, but we've noticed a few things we need to address, and we have someone we'd like to introduce you to."

Another new person? Lily raised an eyebrow in Katie's direction.

"First, I want to say how good most of you are doing with the new requirements. I know it isn't easy to wear a mask all day, but most of you are doing a great job. That being said, we are still seeing some people wearing the mask below their nose or around their chin. It is important that the mask be worn correctly. As you know, we are treading a thin line being open like this, and if we are caught not following the rules, we will be shut down and forced to return to online instruction. Also, some of you are moving chairs closer at lunch. It is especially important during lunch that you stay six feet apart as this is when your mask is down and you are eating. That makes you more susceptible. Along with that, it is important that you put your mask back on as soon as you are finished eating. Finally, we have seen people congregating in the hallways. It is important that we try to keep social distancing measures in place, and for now, that means no hugging and no congregating in hallways."

For now. The words irked Lily. How long had they been hearing them? At first, the people in power had stated these measures were needed for two weeks to flatten the curve. Then, they had said the measures needed to continue to keep the case load down. Now, there were even annoying commercials reminding them that they might be missing birthdays, weddings, and funerals, but that it was only temporary. "Locking down saves lives," the woman on the commercial said, "not forever, but for now." However, it was beginning to feel very much like forever to Lily.

"Now, I'm sure many of you know that we have never had an on-site nurse. However, due to the pandemic, we will this year. Her name is Ms. Dickens, and she is going to discuss some new policies with you."

He stepped back and a woman Lily hadn't noticed before stepped forward. She was dressed all in black, except for the red belt that circled her waist. Her hair was so blonde that it almost appeared white - a stark contrast to her dark clothes. She moved with an effortless grace even though she carried a bulky box under her arm. After setting it on the table, she took the microphone from Mr. Shane and stared out at them. When Mr. Shane stepped away from her, she took off her mask and laid it on the table.

"I'll put that back on as soon as I'm done here, but I wanted to make sure you can all hear what I have to share today. First, it is nice to see you all. I hope I have the pleasure of spending more time with you in the future." Her words were pleasant, but there was something about her voice that sent the hairs on Lily's arms and the back of her neck standing at attention like soldiers in formation. "I see that you all have some face covering, and most of you have masks. That is good. However, it has come to our attention that plastic shields are not beneficial at blocking the virus due to the open sides and bottom. Therefore, we will no longer be allowing them. If you have one, please stay after we are dismissed to pick up a mask from me."

She opened the box and pulled out a surgical mask which she held up. "We will have a box of these in the office and in every classroom. If you forget your mask at any time, you must get one of these to remain on campus. Are there any questions?"

Her eyes scanned the audience, and Lily followed her gaze. A few of the unfortunate students who had been wearing a shield squirmed as her eyes landed on them, but no one raised a hand. Whether that was due to no one having questions or everyone hoping to get out of this room quicker was a toss-up.

"Very well then. The next piece of news I have for you is good news." She smiled out at the crowd, but it did not feel genuine. "I'm sure many of you have been following the news and heard that a wonderful philanthropist named

Daman Caturix planned to use his own money to fund vaccine research."

Lily glanced over at Katie, her eyes wide. Daman Caturix? What did he have to do with this assembly?

"I am pleased to announce that the first vaccine has been approved and because you are in school unlike many of your colleagues, you qualify to get the vaccine right after our first responders."

A girl a few rows over from Lily raised her hand. "What if we don't want the vaccine?" she asked.

Ms. Dicken's eyes darkened for a second, and a chill ran down Lily's spine at the change in her expression. But just as quickly as it came, it was gone, replaced with her forced smile.

"Of course no one will force you to take the vaccine. However, we will not be able to lift the mask and social distance restrictions until everyone in the school is vaccinated. I'm sure none of you want that to continue."

Her eyes roamed the room again, and Lily's heart stopped in her chest when the woman's eyes met hers. She had never felt true evil, but she was fairly certain she was in the presence of it now.

"Now, I have consent forms for each of you that I have given to your principal and your teachers. They will be standing by the exits. Please grab one on your way out. We hope to begin vaccinating in the next few weeks. If you have a mask, you are dismissed to your class. If you do not, please stay here and form an orderly line to receive your mask."

Katie and Lily stood and followed the majority of the students out of the lunchroom. Though she had no desire to take the vaccine, Lily grabbed the form as they passed Mr. Shane. She would make a copy for Gabe and Raven. Maybe it would help them out.

"That was weird, right?" she asked when they were far enough away from listening ears. Lily couldn't even put her finger on what had been so weird about it other than the creepy feeling she got from the new nurse, but her stomach felt like she'd been spun upside down on a roller coaster and left hanging there for a few minutes.

"Yeah, a little. I mean not the words, but…" Katie trailed off as she too struggled to articulate what she felt. "Something felt off. Them pushing the vaccine and almost threatening those who won't take it." Katie turned to Lily, a serious look in her eyes. "Lily, for the first time, I'm really scared."

"Me too," Lily said with a nod. "Me too."

15

Raven looked at the picture on her screen. Lily had sent over a picture of the vaccine consent form, and though Raven knew little about vaccines, she studied the ingredients, looking for anything that might help them understand the rush to make the vaccine and push it out. Especially when deaths were falling.

"Does any of this make sense to you?" Raven asked Gabe as she leaned back, allowing him a better view of the screen.

He scanned the screen, a line furrowing on his forehead as he read.

"What?" Raven asked. "I can tell you see something."

"To be honest, I see a few troubling things, but the first one that stands out is this." He pointed to a line of text about five rows from the top. “Potassium chloride is just a fancy name for salt, but so is sodium chloride. That bothers me. Why have two different types of salt? Then you have Potassium phosphate. It’s in a lot of drugs, but it also carries a long list of side effects including blurred vision, itching or burning sensation, confusion, chest pain, mood changes, vomiting, and seizures.”

Raven whistled softly. “That’s a pretty long list.”

Gabe shook his head. “That’s not even half of it. I don’t know why they would put that in a vaccine at all, but that’s still not what bothers me the most.”

Raven lifted her eyebrows. “It gets worse?”

“Yeah, maybe. It’s the mRNA that bothers me the most.”

“What’s mRNA?” Raven asked.

“It’s hard to describe, but it’s modified RNA. Its goal is to go in and repair RNA. It’s gene therapy, similar to some cancer treatments.”

“Cancer?” Raven leaned forward again. “But NCAV isn’t cancer last I checked. More like the flu.”

“Right, so why would they need to modify our RNA?”

“Could it be a way to keep us from getting NCAV?” Raven knew she was grasping at straws, but she had no idea why the government or Daman Caturix would want to change their RNA.

“I don’t think so,” Gabe said. “It looks like this would actually cause your body to produce the toxin. This could kill people, Raven. Especially those with a weaker immune system to begin with."

"What do you mean?"

"Look, our DNA is perfectly made. When our immune systems are working correctly, it recognizes the bad things and gets rid of them. mRNA is supposed to cling to and modify our DNA so that it will recognize NCAV when we get it and fight it."

"Okay, I don't trust much that comes from the government but that actually sounds like a good thing, right?"

Gabe sighed. "Yes and no. If it works that way, then for a short time it's a good thing. It should lessen the effects of NCAV, but it's modifying DNA and who knows what that's going to do to people in the future. The other, more pressing problem is this. If an immune system thinks the mRNA is bad instead of good, it will fight it, but if it doesn't kill it all, the mRNA will replicate."

Raven suddenly wished she had studied more in science instead of computers. "I'm assuming replication is bad."

"It is. If the DNA fights the RNA and any piece is left, then the next time someone is exposed to anything - flu, cold, whatever, it could be deadly because the immune response will be messed up."

Raven blinked as she tried to process what he was saying. "So, what you're saying is that IF this vaccine works, it might be good in the short term, but we have no idea what the long-term consequences will be, but if it doesn't, we could see this vaccine killing people quickly?"

"Yeah, I'm afraid so."

A moment of tense silence hung between them before Raven shook her head and said, "I don't understand. Why would they want to kill people? I thought that the reason for the masks and the lockdowns was to save as many people as possible."

"I have no idea, but I'll tell you what I do know. We cannot let those girls or Candace or anyone else take that shot if we can help it."

Raven bit the inside of her lip and felt the urge to pray. Though she tried to speak to God every day, so much had begun happening lately that she knew a few days had passed without her praying. However, this news reinforced that prayer right now was more important than ever.

Candace glanced down at her phone. She didn't really have time to take a call right now, but when she saw Raven's number, she knew it had to be important.

"I'll be right back," she said to the nurse on duty, before heading outside. The air was cool outside and instantly sent goosebumps racing up her arms, but it was safer to talk outside. There were fewer listening ears.

"Raven, what's going on?"

"Have you taken the vaccine yet?" Raven asked, jumping straight to the point.

"No, there was some hold up with our doses. They're supposed to be here next week. Why?"

"I know you and Gabe discussed you trying to get access to the vaccines, but it's too dangerous. Lily's school is pressuring the kids to get them, and they sent home the informed consent letter. I'm sending you a copy, but the main ingredient in the vaccine is mRNA."

"mRNA?" Candace asked, "Why would they use that? It's gene therapy."

Raven sighed on the other end. "We don't know. Gabe is looking into it, but he says it isn't safe. He said some could have a reaction to it that could kill them, and even those who don't won't know how it affects them until a few years into the future."

"Yeah, that's definitely strange," Candace said, glancing around to make sure she was still alone. "Gene therapy is only done in extreme cases. It would be like giving radiation therapy to a healthy person. Perhaps this is something they're trying in order to get the vaccine out quicker."

"True, but quicker isn't always better," Raven said. "Look, in the end it's up to you, but Gabe and I are recommending that you don't take the vaccine. Quit if you have to. There's room for you here, and our numbers are growing daily. We could use a good doctor close to home."

Candace took a deep breath and ran a hand through her hair. "I'll think about it. I promise."

After ending the call, Candace shoved the phone back in her pocket, but she didn't return to the ER immediately. Something about the mRNA was nagging the back of her brain, and she decided to clock out for lunch and do some research in her office.

She booted up her computer as she unwrapped her sandwich, but when the screen came to life and the cursor blinked at her, she paused. What exactly was she looking for?

She typed 'effects of mRNA' into the search bar and scrolled through the results. Most were scientific pages desperately claiming there was no adverse effect to mRNA. There were a few less reputable pages claiming that mRNA would modify the DNA and might kill people in the next few years, but it was the few pages hidden among all the others that stood out to Candace. These pages presented the known adverse reactions but stated they were small - one in a million or so, but near the bottom in smaller print was the line that raised the tiny hairs on the back of Candace's neck. Long term effects of mRNA cannot be known, but will be updated next year upon completion of the current trial.

Next year? The government and the media were claiming that the trials had already been done, that the vaccines were safe to take, yet this piece insinuated they were actually still in trial phase and the human population was unknowingly becoming the latest guinea pigs.

'Why, Lord?" she whispered as she scanned the article again. "Why would they subject humans to something this untested for a disease that most survive?"

Daman Caturix. The name flashed like a marquee in her mind, and she typed it into the search bar. She'd never heard of him until a few months ago when he promised to fund the vaccine creation, so she was surprised at how much information there was on him.

Most of the articles were about his philanthropy - the things he'd done since becoming a billionaire to help people. How he became a billionaire was a little harder to find, but it appeared he'd had some luck in the stock markets several years back. Nothing seemed out of the ordinary, and she was about to dismiss him all together when an article caught her eye.

She clicked on it, her eyes widening as she read. "Daman Caturix warns that the Earth is becoming too populated. He asserts that the only way to save the Earth from disaster is a mass reduction in population. When asked how he expected that would come about, his answer was with good vaccines and reproductive care."

Candace read the words over again. Good vaccines and reproductive care would lower the population? That made no sense. She knew his idea of good reproductive care probably meant abortion, and while she didn't agree with the concept, she could see how more abortions would lower the population rate, but good vaccines were supposed to keep people healthier. The only way they would lower the population was if their purpose was not to heal but to sterilize or kill.

A shiver shook her shoulders, and she glanced around the empty room, suddenly feeling as if she was treading in dangerous waters. Her eyes scanned to the end of the piece.

"Daman's final words on the topic are this, 'When a disaster strikes, those who are weakest will embrace the hand that feeds. It will be swift.'"

It will be swift? Not only did the words seem out of context with his previous statement but they possessed a connotation so negative that Candace froze in her chair. Could his vaccine be the means to deliver his swift end? Or could there be even more to it? Regardless, she knew now that she couldn't take that vaccine. And she had to find a way to educate her friends before they took it as well.

16

"Did you watch the news last night?" Katie asked as Lily climbed out of the car. It was Monday morning, the second week of school. In a normal year, this would be the week that everyone settled into their routines and began to adjust to the new year. But this was not a normal year. Not by a long shot.

"I did." Lily couldn't believe she was actually watching the news now, but with everything going on, it felt important to be informed. She felt better knowing she had people like Raven and Pastor Ben on her side, but she was still terrified that the school would try to force her to be vaccinated. She'd heard they couldn't force you to take it, but they could pass mandates limiting your freedom until you did. She was no longer sure which scared her more.

"Do you think he'll close us down again too?"

The governor had held yet another press conference discussing how cases were rising and demanding that college students disband any get-togethers and wear masks even in their dorm rooms. Lily still didn't understand his reasoning. He kept quoting science, but he never showed any. He never showed graphs or listed where this evidence was coming from, yet people all around her lapped it up like it was gospel.

The people at church were some of the only people looking at and discussing real data, and all of that data still showed that students were not at high risk for this virus, and even if they got it, they generally had a very mild case. In fact, the latest reports stated that regardless of age, the survival rate was ninety-five to ninety-nine percent. With numbers like that, Lily still couldn't understand why they were shutting down things to begin with.

"I don't know," she said with a sigh. She'd had high hopes when they started that they would be able to continue the whole year, even if it meant wearing a mask every day, but with each new restriction, she was becoming more convinced they'd be shut down before the end of the first semester.

After getting their temperatures checked, they grabbed their books for science and headed to Mr. Higgins' room. However, his door was closed when they reached the room. That was odd because Mr. Higgins' door was never closed. In fact, Katie and Lily had often debated whether the man slept at the school or not.

"He's not here," a voice said from behind them.

Turning, Lily spied Tristan, a fellow Senior, sitting on the floor with his back against the wall. They must have walked right past him though she had no idea how. "Yeah, that's obvious. You know where he is? He's always here on time."

Tristan whipped his head to move the long brown fringe of bangs out of his eyes. "Heard he got the virus. He'll probably be out for a month at least. If he's lucky."

"What?" Mr. Higgins had seemed fine when they left school on Friday. Plus, he wasn't in the high-risk category. The man was only in his fifties. How could he be out for a month? "How do you know that?"

Tristan shrugged. "Heard them talking about it in the office this morning. Forgot my normal mask and had to borrow one of theirs." He pointed to the surgical mask covering his face.

"Do you know who the sub is?" Katie asked.

Lily could not imagine Mr. Higgins having a sub, especially considering she was pretty sure he made it his personal mission to make their lives as miserable as possible, and she couldn't see him giving that up. Nor could she see anyone teaching his lessons the way he did.

Tristan shrugged and his bangs covered his eyes again. "Yep, heard we have some new guy. That's all I know."

Another new person? With a sigh, Lily slid down to the floor and leaned her back against the wall. Katie followed suit. Neither girl was close with Tristan, but at least he was a human body in this world that suddenly felt very foreign and weird. "This stinks. I hope he's nice."

"Yeah, welcome to this year," Tristan said.

Lily nodded, and for a moment silence descended on the three of them, but it was not one of those comforting silences. It was more like the oppressive kind that left her stomach churning with anxiety. And suddenly she couldn't stand it. "So, how was your summer?"

Tristan flicked his head, sending his bangs swooshing to the side again, and fixed her with intense brown eyes. "What summer? There was nothing to do."

Lily opened her mouth to reply but closed it again. What was she going to say? He was right. Summer had been crappy and fall wasn't shaping up to be much better. Some things had opened for a time like dining inside at restaurants but only with your family. Of course those were closed again now. And gyms had opened but at limited capacity. The press conference last night had shut them down again too. Bowling alleys and movie theaters had opened for a month or two, but masks were mandated the whole time, so she hadn't patroned them when they were open. Like everything else, they had been forced to close their doors again as well.

Suddenly, the sound of footsteps interrupted the

awkward silence that had fallen between the students. Lily glanced up to see an imposing figure approaching, his loafers tapping on the linoleum floor. He was tall and thin, reminding her a little of Thin Man, the character on some video games meant to scare kids. His black hair was perfectly placed, and dark eyes peered over his mask. A tiny thread of fear erupted in her stomach, and she swallowed to keep it down. He was just a man, a dark and sinister looking man, but a man just the same.

"Ah, the eager beavers. I do like seeing that."

Even his voice set her on edge. What was it about all these new adults? Why did every one of them give her such a foreboding feeling? Sneaking a glance at Tristan, she saw his face was still focused on the phone in his lap. Katie's eyes, however, were wide and fearful, and Lily believed hers looked similar.

"I'm Mr. Dagon, and I'll be your science teacher now." He unlocked the door and pushed it into place so that it stayed open before ushering them inside.

"Wait, now? I thought Mr. Higgins was just home sick. He's coming back, right?"

"What? Oh, of course he is. I mean that I'll be your science teacher until he returns."

Mr. Dagon's demeanor still appeared confident, but Lily had heard the hitch in his voice, some hint of emotion that left her wondering if Mr. Higgins would return.

When Mr. Dagon flicked on the light switch, Lily

nearly dropped her bag. She blinked at the room as another round of trepidation passed through her. Mr. Higgins had always had the room decorated in bright colors with lots of natural light, but now it was dark. The windows were covered with some film that only let in the softest gray color. Dark posters hung around the room, and the only other word she could grasp at the moment to describe the place was sterile. Empty, sterile, and dark. She had never been in a morgue, but suddenly she was sure it would feel exactly like this. How on earth had he transformed the room so quickly? And why, if he was only subbing for a week or so?

"What happened here?" The words escaped Lily's mouth before she could stop them, and as soon as his head whipped her direction and his eyes bore into hers, she knew she had made a mistake.

"If I am to be working here for the foreseeable future, then it only makes sense the room should be to my liking. Now, pick your desk," Mr. Dagon said, "but be sure to choose wisely. Whatever desk you choose right now is the one you will remain in for the entirety of class. I will not be cleaning desks willy nilly."

Lily turned her wide eyes to Katie. Though she said nothing, she hoped that Katie would understand her silent question. Why had a substitute redecorated Mr. Higgins' room? And why was he acting as if they'd be there all day instead of just the fifty minutes for the first period?

Katie offered a small shrug and a subtle shake of her head in response. It wasn't much, but it let Lily know that she had understood the question and that she had no answer either.

As Lily walked to the desk she had used last week, she noticed new tape marks on the floor. She'd performed in a few plays over the years and had marked stages for set pieces. The tape had never seemed threatening or dark before. But it did now. The once bright room now looked like an elaborate tragedy with all the desks exactly six feet apart.

Katie leaned close and whispered. "What happened here? It feels so cold."

Lily shook her head, but it did not ease the fear that this might only be the beginning. First, the vaccine push on Friday and now this. Deep down, she supposed she knew this day would come. After the rapture, it was only a matter of time before the Antichrist was revealed, and he tried to take over the world. Lily just hadn't thought it would come so soon.

She took a small comfort in knowing she was not alone in her unease. Though everyone who entered was masked, she could see the shock play across their eyes as they stepped into the room. Most were too timid to ask any questions. Connor, unfortunately, was not.

"Whoa," he said as he slid into the classroom right before the bell went off. "Who are you and what happened to Mr. Higgins?" Connor was the typical jock. He almost always wore jerseys of some sort - basketball, football, hockey. Lily had never seen him in anything else, and she wasn't sure he owned other types of shirts. Plus, he was a little cocky and loud. That worked in his favor during most sports games, but it did nothing for him with Mr. Dagon.

Mr. Dagon looked up from his computer and fixed Connor with an icy glare. "Mr. Higgins will be out for a few weeks. I am Mr. Dagon, and in my class, we don't have verbal outbursts like that."

Connor shrugged as he plopped into the last unoccupied desk. "The bell just rang, dude."

Lily had seen teachers get upset before. In fact, she'd seen them get upset at Connor before, but she'd never seen such hatred pour forth from a teacher's eyes like the kind that issued now from Mr. Dagon. "I am not your dude, young man. You will address me with respect, and to make up for your poor behavior, you will stay after class to sanitize the desks today."

Though Connor offered another shrug, Lily saw the muscles in his back tighten. He didn't like being called out and receiving punishment was even worse.

"Good, now that expectations are settled, we can begin class. Let's begin by researching and discussing the effectiveness of vaccines."

"But we don't have the vaccine yet," came a small voice from behind Lily.

"We will soon," Mr. Dagon said as his eyes swept over the room. "We will soon."

"Aren't you coming?"

Candace glanced up from her salad to see one of the older nurses, Anne, in the doorway. Anne was probably only in her late fifties, but her graying hair made her appear older. Still, she was one of Candace's favorite nurses to work with. She was kind but a hard worker, and she could switch from spitting out nails to issuing soothing words like a grandmother on the turn of a dime.

"No, I'm going to finish eating first," Candace said. She'd had to work through lunch and was just now getting a chance to eat. She hadn't planned it, but it had come as a welcome excuse to not take the first round of vaccines that were being pushed on the medical staff.

"Have you eaten? Do you want to join me?" She'd tried to convince Anne not to get the vaccine, but for all her good qualities, Anne's downfall was that she truly believed the government was there to help everyone.

"Don't tell me you believe those conspiracy theories," Anne had said when Candace had brought up the issue. "I think you might need more sleep."

"It's not a conspiracy theory if it's true," Candace had pressed, but Anne had merely shaken her head and claimed she was doing it

not only for herself but for her husband who was diabetic. They'd been living apart for the past several months and Anne wanted to be able to go home to him.

Candace could certainly understand that as there wasn't a day that went by that she didn't miss her own husband. Still, she worried for Anne. She knew not everyone would have an immediate adverse reaction. Some might not have one at all, but she'd been checking the site daily that posted them and the increasing number gave her even more hesitation.

"No, I ate earlier," Anne said, answering Candace's question. Candace couldn't see her smile, but the crinkle lines on the sides of her eyes led her to believe the woman smiled behind her mask. "Thank you for asking though. I know you have misgivings, but I hope that you'll see after today that this vaccine is safe."

"I hope so too," Candace said, but she knew in her gut that wouldn't be the case. As Anne left the room, Candace sent up a prayer for her safety and for all the other people who were taking the vaccine believing they were doing the right thing. "Please protect them, Lord."

Raven entered the large warehouse behind Pastor Ben and Nathan and smiled. Though it was just a large space now, it would be perfect if they ever needed it. "This is amazing. Where did you find this place?"

Nathan stuck out his chest and smiled broadly. "My next-door neighbor owned it. He said he and wife had planned on opening a company but then she disappeared. He told me about it one night when I was witnessing to him and said he had no use for it anymore. I asked if he'd be obliged to sell it, and he agreed."

"Thankfully, the church still had funds in our account from before the rapture, and we've been receiving modest tithes from those who've attended after," Ben added. "We were able to reach a deal with Nathan's neighbor."

Raven stepped forward and scanned the area. There were a few office areas, a break room which she assumed held a sink and a fridge, and a bathroom. With a few other partitions, she could envision a place where many would be able to live more or less comfortably. It would be like a large commune, but it would be better than being isolated. A part of her still hoped this wouldn't be necessary, but with the vaccines hitting the streets already, she knew it would be.

"This is great," she said, smiling at them. "Will we be able to get some partitions and beds and maybe a few showers?"

Nathan smiled again. "Yep, I'm already working on that with some fellows from the church. Thankfully, we have a few contractors and plumbers among our congregation now, and they have offered their services."

Raven placed a hand on Nathan's shoulder. "That is

wonderful news, Nathan. You are doing more than you know for all of us."

The man blushed and dropped his eyes to the floor. "Aw, thanks, but I'm just happy to be doing the work of the Lord. It's something I should have been doing a long time ago."

"We all should have been," Pastor Ben said, speaking up. "I'm working with some of the parishioners who like to garden as well. We've got a few acres here, but unfortunately it's going to take us a bit to have a sustainable garden."

Raven nodded. She worried about that. So far, they were still allowed to shop, and she made sure to purchase extra items whenever she went, but she knew the day was coming when that would no longer be an option. At least not unless Gabe could work a miracle and find a way to forge their vaccination documents.

"How is our pantry looking? Do you think it will hold us over until then?"

Ben ran a hand across his chin. "It's growing every day, but so are our numbers. If the crackdown comes too soon, I worry. We need another few months at least before I will feel comfortable."

"We'll pray we get that then. How about our sister churches? Have they been as lucky as we have at finding resources?"

Ben nodded. "Some more than others, but all have a

pantry and a few others have secured a building such as ours. I'll keep reminding them how pressing this issue is."

"As will I in the next video I do," Raven said. "I'm glad that more people are waking up, but I hope God gives us some time to prepare."

"Me too." The gravity in Ben's voice mirrored the weight on Raven's shoulders, but there was only one thing she could do. Pray.

17

"Okay, it's weird, right?" Katie asked Lily as she unwrapped her sandwich. She was on one end of the table and Lily was on the other. Though the girls sat at a table that could hold three students, it was just the two of them today.

Lily glanced around the cafeteria and realized it did seem sparser. Were there students missing? She'd heard rumors of a few students having to quarantine, but that had only been one or two. It seemed more like ten or more were missing, so, where were they?

"Lunch or everything else?" she asked. Weird did not begin to describe everything that she was feeling. The morning had been so odd that she was having a hard time even unpacking it all in her head.

First, there had been science - another day with the

creepy Mr. Dagon leaning over their shoulders as they researched and continually interrupting them with a random fact about the efficacy of vaccines. Lily was beginning to think he was on payroll with the pharmaceutical companies as much as he pushed the idea. He'd even asked them how many of them had returned their forms and were looking forward to their shots in the next week or so. Lily and Katie had exchanged a glance but kept their mouths closed. There was no need to draw unneeded attention to themselves. That day would come soon enough.

After science, she'd enjoyed a reprieve with a slightly normal English class with Mrs. Fox. Mrs. Fox was normally one of her favorite teachers, but today she, as well as the history teacher Ms. Turnbull, had seemed off. Both women were normally vivacious and chatty, but today their normal animation had appeared forced. Maybe it was the influx of new substitutes. Lily knew the teachers at this school were almost as close as the students, and not only was Mr. Higgins gone, but the math teacher had also been replaced. Supposedly, she was on a two-week quarantine, but Lily was beginning to have her doubts.

The math sub wasn't as creepy as Mr. Dagon or Ms. Dickens, but she didn't seem especially friendly either. Dressed all in black, her pale skin had appeared even more white, giving her the look of Morticia or Wendy Addams.

Her tone had been monotonous as she droned on about the assignment and her class expectations while Ms. Owings was out.

"All of it. Like where did Mr. Higgins and Ms. Owings go? Are they really sick? If so, why hasn't the government shut us down? I was reading the opening plan again the other night, after we met the new nurse, and it said that more than one case would be considered an outbreak and could shut us down again. Yet now we supposedly have two teachers and several students out and we're business as usual?"

Lily bit the inside of her lip and looked around again. "Yeah, the whole thing is strange, but maybe they don't actually have the virus. Maybe they were just exposed and had to quarantine. Or maybe they both got tired of teaching with a mask on. I can barely breathe in mine, and I don't talk much during class. I can't imagine having to teach with one on." She glared at the folded piece of fabric on the side of her table. Thankfully, students were still allowed to take their masks off to eat, but they were required to put them on as soon as they finished their lunch. Lily had never been an especially slow eater, but she was finding a way to drag out her eating lately. Her face still felt hot and itchy from the mask, and she dreaded putting it back on after lunch.

Katie popped a chip in her mouth and chewed. When her mouth was clear, she picked up the conversation again.

"I suppose that's possible, but I feel like the school should have said something about it. And what's with these substitute teachers they hired? They're so…" she shuddered, "impersonal. One of the things I loved about going here was that the teachers seemed to care. The new ones feel cold."

Cold was a good word. Everything felt so odd this year, but cold definitely summed up the subs well.

"But I didn't do anything." The loud, protesting voice grabbed the girls' attention, and they turned to see Connor facing off with Mr. Dagon. Connor was one of those kids who spent a lot of time in the principal's office - not usually for anything major, but he had a way of not following the rules just enough to get in trouble. Usually, it was for being late or mouthing off in class. Lily wondered what it was this time.

"You will come with me or you won't be returning tomorrow." Mr. Dagon's low voice held the note of authority that seemed to sober Connor. With a roll of his eyes, Connor followed the new teacher out of the lunch room and toward the office.

"Can he do that?" Katie asked. "Kick him out of school for not coming with him?"

Lily shrugged. She didn't even know what Connor had done this time. The buzz in the lunch room was loud, but not so loud that the students hadn't heard the exchange. However, there had been no disruption beforehand, which made her wonder exactly what Connor was in trouble for.

"I don't know, but I don't plan on finding out for myself. Maybe he didn't do a good job cleaning the desks this morning."

After mouthing off the other day, Mr. Dagon had required Connor to clean the desks every day for the next two weeks. Lily had never been a troublemaker, but it appeared toeing the line would be more important than ever this year. Spending extra time with Mr. Dagon was about the worst punishment she could imagine.

The bell rang a few minutes later, and with a sigh, she replaced her mask before gathering up her trash to throw it away. Just three more hours, she told herself, but three hours felt like a lifetime.

When the final bell rang, relief flooded her body. She could not wait to get out of this building, rip the mask off, and breathe in fresh air. Could she really do this for the rest of the year? Another hundred and fifty plus days?

"Hey, did you see Connor after lunch?" Katie asked as she met up with Lily outside the classroom door.

Lily shook her head. "No, why?"

"I don't know. He was just acting really weird."

Lily lifted an eyebrow at Katie. "Connor is often weird. I'm afraid you'll have to be more specific."

Katie glanced around as if afraid of someone overhearing her words. "You know how he got called out by Mr. Dagon at lunch?"

Lily nodded as the girls continued toward their lockers. Katie's eyes darted around again. Though not generally a nervous person, Katie's behavior was turning Lily into one at the moment. Suddenly, she felt the hairs on the back of her neck rise as if someone was watching them. Lily's eyes darted around as well, but she saw no one.

Katie scanned the area one more time before continuing. Her voice was barely above a whisper this time though and Lily had to strain to discern the words from behind her mask. "Well, when he came into last period, he was all weird, like spacey or something. His eyes were kind of glazed over, and he just sat there quietly and did what he was told."

Okay, that was more than a little weird. Connor wasn't a "bad" kid, but he was definitely not the type of student who sat and did what he was told in class. His name was usually uttered no fewer than five times along with the words "focus" or "get to work." For him to actually do that without reminders was odd.

Lily opened her locker and exchanged the no-longer needed books for her backpack. "Well, maybe he got in enough trouble for whatever he did that he decided to focus."

Katie leaned up against the lockers and folded her arms. "Maybe, but something about the whole thing bothers me."

Lily had no argument there. The first few weeks of

Senior year might be in the books but it was certainly the weirdest start of school she'd ever had. "Yeah." She shut the locker, and the two headed toward the front entrance. "You want to get together later?"

"Sure, I can swing by after dinner."

"Okay, sounds good."

Twenty minutes later, Lily pulled into the driveway of her house. She grabbed her mask from the seat where she'd thrown it, determined to now wash it daily.

During all of their required vaccine research, Lily had stumbled across an old article that stated the majority of the deaths of 1918 had come not from the flu but from bacterial pneumonia after the fact. Bacterial pneumonia that had sprouted on the masks the people had been forced to wear.

This knowledge made Lily hate the masks even more, and a part of her feared she might be damaging her lungs by wearing one all day. However, she was determined to try and get a quality education, so if that meant washing it every day to keep the bacteria at bay, she would do that. In addition, she had begun taking Vitamin D and Zinc after Gabe and Raven recommended them.

"How was school today?" Her mother asked as she entered the kitchen. She sat at the table, her laptop open in front of her.

"It was interesting." Lily dropped her bag by the chair before heading to the pantry to find a snack.

"What do you mean interesting?"

Grabbing a packet of fruit snacks from the shelf, Lily tore the package open and popped one in her mouth before answering. "Well, wearing a mask all day still stinks for one thing." She ran her hand across her chin. There was still some weird phantom feeling there even after nearly half an hour with no mask on.

"Okay, but that will get better with time. What else?"

Lily pulled out the chair across from her mother and sat down. "We've had a bunch of new hires at school. A new counselor, a new nurse, and now we have a few substitutes. The school told us the teachers who are out got sick, but I don't know. Regardless, the subs and the new hires aren't nearly as friendly."

Lines of concern creased her mother's forehead. "Well, this is probably new territory for them too. Give them time. I'm sure it will get better."

Lily shrugged. Though she highly doubted that, she wasn't in the mood to argue with her mother over it. Besides, there was nothing she could do except not go to school and that certainly wasn't an option. At least not until they required the vaccine.

"Oh, by the way, I signed this for you," her mother said, sliding a sheet of paper across the table.

Lily glanced down at it and shook her head. "No way. I'm not taking it, Mom."

"Lily." Her mother's voice took on that condescending

tone that Lily couldn't stand. "I know you've been reading conspiracy websites that claim it isn't safe, but everything I've seen says it is. Besides, it's the only way we can get back to normal, remember?"

Lily stared at her mother. What had happened to her? Her mother no longer attended church, but she hadn't seemed like the type to buy everything the government pushed hook, line, and sinker either. Now, she was not only dismissing Lily's fears but pushing the idea of back to normal? Her mother was beginning to sound like the commercials Lily hated.

"I don't think they'll ever let us get back to normal," Lily mumbled.

Her mother placed a hand on her arm. "Now, honey, I know it's been hard, but this will pass. Things might not go back to exactly the way they were before, but this will help."

"Mom, do you hear yourself? Dr. Goodman was on the TV last night saying that even after we get this vaccine, we still have to wear a mask and be socially distant. He said we could still even catch NCAV, and now they're talking about a new strain being discovered? This will never end."

Lily had never spoken to her mother like that, and for a moment she thought about apologizing, but then she remembered Raven saying their job was to spread the word, show people the truth, wake them up. Who better to start with than her mother?

"Lily, I…" her mother sputtered like a car trying to start on a cold morning.

"Mom, I love you, but I need you to listen to me now." Lily waited for her mother to agree. Then she took a deep breath and began to share everything she knew.

Candace had just stepped out of the on-call room when Julia came running up to her.

"Dr. Markham, you have to come quickly," Julia said, grabbing her arm and pulling her toward the farthest exam room.

"What is it?" Candace asked, fighting the urge to dislodge Julia's grip on her arm. Clearly, something had scared her. Julia was generally a level-headed nurse even though she was on the younger side, but right now, she looked as if the ghost of her dead grandmother had just walked through the walls of the hospital.

Julia glanced around before answering in a hushed whisper, "It's Anne."

"Anne? What's wrong with Anne?" As soon as the words left her mouth, Candace remembered the vaccine station yesterday and how proud Anne was to be getting the vaccine even after Candace warned her not to. "Oh no."

She quickened her pace and followed Julia into the last ER room on the floor. Anne lay in the bed, her body convulsing. It presented like a seizure except much more frequent and instead of glazed eyes, Anna's fearful ones were fixed on Candace. "What's happening to me?"

"I don't know, Anne, but I promise you I will find out. When did this start?"

"Last night." She paused as her head shook uncontrollably, flopping from one side to the other. "I felt weird after the shot, so I took the rest of the day off." Another pause as the shaking pulsed down her body. "It started with my foot. Just jerking on its own. Then the other one." She paused again as her arm lifted off the bed before flopping back down. "I took some Tylenol PM to help me sleep, but when I woke up this morning, it was worse."

"Okay, I'm going to run some tests and do some research. Just try to relax." Candace squeezed Anne's arm and offered a sympathetic smile. She wished she could do more, but the vaccine was so new that few side effects had even been reported and nothing like this. She did know that she had to do more. Regardless of what happened with her job, she needed to start speaking out about this vaccine so that no one else ended up like Anne.

18

The next morning Lily pulled into the school parking lot and sighed. She'd checked her bag twice before she left to make sure she had everything, but it appeared her mask had been forgotten. It was probably still in the dryer as she washed them daily now, hoping to avoid bacterial pneumonia. There wasn't time to go back for it without being late, so she decided to just grab one of the ones the school was handing out. She wasn't the first one to have to use one, and she doubted she would be the last. High schoolers were notorious for losing things.

After locking the car, she headed for the temperature check in point, stifling another sigh when she saw that Mr. Dagon was the teacher on that duty today. Just her luck.

Pasting her best smile on, she sucked in a deep breath and approached him.

He held up his hand to signal her to stop when she was a good six feet from him. "Where's your mask?"

"I forgot it at home, but the nurse said the school has extras. Can I just grab one of those?"

His eyes raked over her as if he was trying to assess if she was lying or not. Weird since she couldn't imagine lying about something so silly. Masks were bad enough when they were your own, but why would anyone want to borrow one from the school?

"You do know that a face covering is a requirement every day?"

It took every ounce of self-control not to roll her eyes at him. "Yes, I do. I washed it last night because it was making my face itch, and I forgot to grab it from the dryer this morning. I can't guarantee it will never happen again, but I'll certainly do my best."

"Fine. Wait there." He disappeared into the building and returned a moment later with a plain surgical mask. As if afraid he would catch something from her, he held it out delicately, the ear loop dangling between two fingers.

Grabbing it, she slipped it on before continuing forward to get her temperature checked.

"Do you have any of these symptoms?" he asked, turning the clipboard toward her.

Lily shook her head. She wouldn't have answered yes even if she did because some of the symptoms were stupid. Headache? She got one often if she didn't eat soon enough or if she stayed up too late. Cough? Yep, if she ran in cold weather, she had one that stuck around for a few hours after.

"Have you been exposed to anyone who has NCAV?"

"Not that I know of," Lily said, unable to keep the condescension out of her voice.

Mr. Dagon glared at her a moment but finally stepped away from the door, allowing her to enter.

As she stepped into the building, a wave of dizziness rolled over her. Lily placed her hand against the wall to steady herself and blinked a few times as the hall in front of her swam. She took a few deep breaths, but each one amplified the fuzzy sensation in her head. She stumbled down the hall to the nearest doorway and leaned into it, hoping Mr. Dagon wouldn't see her. Then she lowered her mask and took a few more deep breaths. It wasn't immediate, but after a few minutes, the strange sensation strangling her softened its hold.

"What was that?" she whispered under her breath. She glanced around, and after confirming she was alone, she slipped off the surgical mask and examined it. Nothing appeared off. It looked just like every other disposable mask. Maybe it was a reaction to the fabric? Her normal ones were cloth and softer. Could she have an allergy to something in the disposable mask? If so, would she have to go home or would it be something that would go away after time?

She replaced the mask and took a tentative breath. It smelled different from her cloth masks, a sort of plastic scent, but nothing out of the ordinary. Shaking her head, she continued down the hall to her locker.

Katie appeared a moment later. "What's with the surgical mask?" she asked, holding out a coffee.

"I forgot mine at home. This is what they loan you, remember?"

Her brows furrowed for a moment. "Huh, I thought the ones Ms. Dickens showed us were light blue. That one looks darker."

Lily shrugged. "Maybe it was from a different batch. Darker dye?"

"Yeah, maybe, well anyway, stylish," she said as she leaned her back against the locker next to Lily's.

"Yeah, not really, but it saved me from having to drive home. I think it might let more air in too. My breath doesn't feel quite as hot on my face. I might have to see if I can get some more of these."

Katie's brow lifted on her forehead. "More of them? Why? You hate masks. Why on earth would you want more of them?"

"I don't know. This one doesn't seem as bad. Maybe I wouldn't mind them so much if I had one like this."

Tiny wrinkles erupted on Katie's forehead as her

brows knitted together. "Are you feeling okay? He did take your temperature at the door, didn't he?"

"Yes, he did, and I feel fine." Lily grabbed the last book she needed and shut the locker door, only to find Katie staring at her with concerned eyes. "What? I'm fine. Let's get to class."

"You know what? I have an extra mask in my bag. Why don't you use it instead?" She dropped her backpack from her shoulders and rummaged around in it.

"Katie, I'm fine. The smell is a little weird, but other than that, it's not that bad."

"Smell? What smell? In the mask?"

"Yeah, I think so, unless you smell it too."

Katie shook her head. "I don't smell anything unusual."

"Ooh, maybe it's because this one seems to let in more air. Maybe the school is trying a new sanitizing agent, and you can't smell it because the cloth on your mask is so thick. I mean it did make me feel a little dizzy at first, but I feel fine now."

"You were dizzy?" Katie asked.

"Yeah, had to hold on to the wall for a few minutes. Felt like I was in a fun house with the hallway tilting, but it's gone now. Hey, maybe the new antiseptic will work so well that we'll be able to stop wearing masks. I was watching this article on the news the other day that said airplane filters were so good that even if someone next to you wasn't wearing their mask, you wouldn't get sick. Maybe they found something like that for schools."

"I doubt it." Katie looked around and then lowered her mask.

"What are you doing?" Lily glanced back toward the front entrance where Mr. Dagon was still taking temperatures. "You're going to get in trouble." Suddenly, she felt sure that not only would he see them, but that he would be very angry if he caught them with their masks down.

"Sniffing." She made a show of sniffing the air and shaking her head. "Take your mask down. I don't smell anything."

"I'm not taking it off. Are you crazy? Mr. Dagon is right outside, and I have no desire to be hauled to the principal like Connor yesterday."

"Are you listening to yourself?" Katie asked. "You... hate... the... mask." She punctuated each word as if it was a sentence on its own.

"It's really not that bad." Lily blinked. Had she just said that? The girl who ripped the mask off as soon as she stepped out of the school? Why did it all of a sudden not seem so bad?

"Come on." Katie put her mask back in its place, threw her backpack back over her shoulder, and grabbed Lily's arm. A minute later, she pushed open the bathroom door and shoved Lily into the handicapped stall, locking the door behind her.

"What are you doing?" Lily asked.

"You are changing masks. I don't know what they did to that, but something is wrong with it." She unzipped her backpack, dug around some more, and finally held out a spare mask.

"Really, I'm fine." Lily took a step back, colliding with the cold metal of the stall. Her hand waved off the mask Katie held out, but in her head a tiny alarm bell began to blare. She said she was fine, and she felt fine, but if she was really fine then why was an alarm going off? What was her body trying to tell her?

Like a sneaky fox, Katie snatched the mask from Lily's face. "You are not fine. You're acting all agreeable to this nonsense, and it's scaring me, so you will wear this." She held out her spare mask.

For a moment, Lily wanted to protest. She opened her mouth to demand her mask back, but before she could say a word, she'd forgotten what she wanted to say. The words that had been there only a moment before now dissipated like fog in the morning. Lily blinked and shook her head a few times before focusing on her friend. "What was that for?"

"I think there's something on this," Katie said, folding the mask carefully and placing it in her purse.

"Katie, I think you've been watching too much TV. There's nothing on the mask."

"I don't believe that. Tell me, do you smell the new cleaner now?"

Lily wrinkled her nose in disgust. "We're in the bathroom. I'm not sucking in a lungful right now."

"Well, I can tell you that you won't. Something on this mask was affecting you, and I'm going to find out what. We'll take it to Raven and Gabe this afternoon. Until then, wear mine. How did you forget yours anyway? I thought you kept it in your car."

"I did until I read that article about bacterial pneumonia. Now I wash it every day, and I left it in the dryer."

"Then keep a spare in your car. You cannot take a mask from here again."

"You have seriously lost it," Lily said, but she grabbed the mask Katie offered.

"That's fine. You can think I'm crazy until I can prove it to you, but better safe than sorry." She zipped up her purse and checked her watch. "We better get to class, but let's keep an eye on anybody else wearing these masks. I want to see if everyone is affected like you were."

Suddenly Katie's words about Connor the previous day flooded Lily's mind. "Hey, Katie, was Connor wearing one of these masks when you thought he was acting weird yesterday?"

Her lips twisted to the side as she thought. "I don't remember, but it's possible. It would certainly explain his behavior."

"Yeah, maybe." Lily still wasn't sure anything was wrong with the mask, but with this year, she was keeping an open mind.

Candace stared at her phone unsure exactly what to say. She looked back at Anne who still shook uncontrollably in the bed. "Are you sure you want to do this, Anne?"

"I'm sure," Anne said as a tear escaped the corner of her eye. "You were right, and I should have listened. If I had known this could happen, it might have changed my mind. There may not be hope for me, but perhaps we can save others from the same fate."

Candace nodded and squeezed her friend's arm. She hated that not only was Anne in this position, but that she seemed unable to help her. She would not give up though. Not until she found a cure.

After taking a deep breath, Candace hit the record button. "My name is Dr. Candace Markham. Many of you will not know me, but I'm an ER doctor in Washington state. I have been on the front lines of NCAV, but I have remained silent, and for that I am sorry. Some of you have spoken out about this virus and you have been demonized and canceled. I said nothing, but I am speaking now. NCAV is real, but it is not as dangerous as the media has led you to believe. Most patients recover, especially if they are given Ramidil, a treatment we used in the beginning until we were told to stop. I have continued to treat my patients with it as have other doctors, but I know many of you lost your jobs when you refused to comply.

"In addition, we were told to inflate the number of deaths. Any person who expired in this hospital was tested for NCAV and if they were positive, even though it was not their cause of death, they were listed as an NCAV death. I know for a fact that our numbers are inflated in the hundreds. I can only assume if my hospital is, then others across the country are as well which means the numbers could be inflated in the thousands. I knew this was wrong, but again I didn't speak out because I didn't think it was that big of a deal.

"However, now I understand why it was. Now I understand why the media had to drum the fear of this virus up even if they did it by fudging the numbers. It was so you would take their vaccine. Now, I'm going to be honest, I hadn't done a lot of research on this vaccine until a few days ago, but I am convinced that no one should take this vaccine. There are many reasons, but let me just share one."

Candace moved closer to the bed and held the camera out so that Anne would be included in the shot. "This is my friend, Anne. She took the vaccine a few days ago and the next morning, her body began to shake. It started small with just her foot, but now, as you can see, her body shakes uncontrollably. She is not faking this, and at this point, I don't know what's wrong with her or how to treat it. Please, if you won't believe me, do some research on the vaccine. Look into mRNA and watch the other doctors who were braver than me and put out videos much earlier."

Candace moved her finger to end the video, but then she was struck with one more thing. It was reckless to say it, but so was everything else she had just said, so she might as well go big. "One last thing. The disappearances that happened months ago were not from aliens or Russia. That was the rapture. Those of us who remain were left behind and if you're not up on your Bible theology, what comes next is the Tribulation. I believe we are in those times and it will probably only get worse. Find a Bible, find a church, go to TruthSeekers.org and learn. We may not have much time left, but we can save our souls."

She pressed the button to stop recording and turned to Anne. "I'm sorry. I didn't mean to get preachy at the end, but I can't be silent any longer."

"Do you really believe what you said?" Anne asked, reaching out her hand.

Candace took it and nodded. "I do."

"Then I want to as well. Tell me what to do."

Candace smiled and reached for the nearby chair. She

had let her friend down once, but perhaps she could give her the best gift of all.

"I'm so glad today is over, but I don't know how I'm going to avoid this vaccine," Katie said as the girls put their books away for the day and grabbed their bags.

"Me either," Lily said. "My mom doesn't believe me when I tell her it might be dangerous. Do you think we'll have to leave?"

"Leave our parents?"

"If we have to," Lily said and shut her locker door. "Look, I don't like it either, but Raven is working on a place for everyone in the future if they force the vaccination. We can always go there."

"Yeah, I suppose you're right-"

The sound of violent retching cut her off, and the girls looked toward the staff lounge where the noise appeared to be coming from. The room, while for the teachers, was rarely closed as it also held the copy machine and the extra supplies. Except for during lunch, the door was generally propped open, and the blinds covering the small window were open. Now, however, both were very much closed, but someone was clearly in there. Someone who sounded as if they needed help.

"Do we check it out?" The trepidation in Katie's voice matched the feeling racing through Lily's body.

"I don't know." A part of her thought they should. After all, it was the nice thing to do. If she was sick, she'd want someone to check on her. But there was this part, this tiny voice in her head, that was screaming this was a bad idea and they should just leave.

Before either of them could decide, the door opened, and Mr. Dagon stepped out. His eyes widened as he caught sight of them. "What are you doing here?"

"We were on our way out," Katie said in a shaky voice, "and we heard someone vomiting. Was it you? Are you okay?"

For a split second, a look of fear or anger flashed in Mr. Dagon's eyes, but as quickly as it appeared, it was gone, and his cool demeanor was back in place. "Yes, sorry, I swallowed something that didn't agree with me. I'm sorry to have alarmed you. All is well."

But all didn't feel well to Lily. For one thing, he still seemed a little nervous. For another, she wasn't sure she bought his story. Vomiting was considered a symptom of the virus. Could he be sick and trying to hide it? While that was possible, what bothered her the most was that he kept the door closed behind him. As if he was hiding something or someone. She wanted to push the issue, but the voice in her head roared louder.

LEAVE!

"Okay, well, glad to know you're okay. See you tomorrow." Lily grabbed Katie's arm and pulled her toward the exit, not daring to look back until they reached the front door. As she pushed on the metal bar, she spared a final glance, only to see Mr. Dagon still standing in the same spot, watching them. The creepy image reminded her of an Edgar Allan Poe story, and she quickly turned away.

"What was that about?" Katie asked when the door closed behind them.

"I don't know, but that was NOT normal."

Katie sighed. "I'm not sure I even remember what normal feels like anymore."

Lily knew that feeling all too well.

"Lily, Katie, you okay?" Raven stepped back and ushered the two girls in. The fear on their faces sent her own heart thundering in her chest.

"We're okay," Lily said. "We just had a weird experience at our school."

"Do you want to tell me what happened?" Raven didn't relate to the teenagers as well as some of the others did, but she could tell they were shaken up.

"In a minute," Katie said, her eyes darting around the room. "Is Gabe here? We have something we need him to examine."

Raven nodded and hollered for Gabe. He entered a moment later.

"Hey, Lily, Katie. What can I do for you?"

Katie dug in her bag and pulled out a surgical mask. "Can you see if there's anything on this? Lily forgot her mask this morning and this is what they gave her, but she said it made her dizzy."

"Dizzy, hmm?" Gabe asked as he reached for the mask. "Did you have any other issues?"

"It smelled funny," Lily said, "and Katie said I acted weird."

"She did," Katie interrupted. "She said the mask wasn't so bad, and she hates masks."

"Okay, well let me run some tests on it. I'll be back in a bit." Gabe took the mask and disappeared down the hallway.

"Now, do you guys want to tell me what else happened?" Raven asked, pointing to the couch and inviting them to sit down.

Lily and Katie exchanged a glance before Lily began, "We've had a few new teachers join our school. They tell us they're subs for teachers who got NVAC, but…"

"But they're strange," Katie said, interrupting. "This one teacher, Mr. Dagon is the worst. He keeps having us research how effective vaccines are, and today -"

"Wait," Raven said, holding up a hand and interrupting Katie. "Did you say Dagon?"

"Yeah, why?"

"Dagon was mentioned in the Bible. He was the father of Baal."

"Whoa, that's creepy," Lily said. "So, he was like an idol in the Bible."

Raven nodded. "Sorry to interrupt you, but I think you need to be very careful around this man."

The girls exchanged another uncomfortable glance. "Well, that brings us to today's event. As we were leaving school, we heard what sounded like someone throwing up in the staff lounge. We weren't sure if we should check it out, but I had a bad feeling. Before we could decide, Mr. Dagon opened the door. He seemed shocked to see us but told us it was him throwing up, except he didn't look sick. Then I heard a voice in my head that said leave, so we got out of there."

Raven bit the inside of her lip. She didn't want to tell the girls to leave school - theirs was one of the few actually open - but she was concerned for their safety. "Is there any way you both can avoid him?"

"He's our first period teacher, at least until our regular teacher returns," Katie said with a shake of her head, "so, I don't see how."

"Well, then how about staying together. Can you make sure you are never alone?"

The girls looked at each other again. "Yeah," Lily finally said, "we have several of our classes together anyway, and the ones we don't, we have other friends in. We can make sure we go nowhere alone."

"Good, do that. Hopefully, it will turn out to be nothing, but I don't want to take any chances."

"You said you got this from your school?" Gabe asked, re-entering the room.

"Yeah, why?" Lily asked.

"I found traces of Methylene Chloride on it. It was small but enough to be the cause of your dizziness and confusion. I can't believe they would give you a mask like this."

"The question is... did they know?" Raven asked. She looked at the girls and then at Gabe. "Either someone at the school did this on purpose or the manufacturer of the masks did."

The insinuation of those words fell heavy on the group. What evil were they dealing with?

19

"Dr. Markham, I need to have a word with you."

Candace looked up to see Dr. Aikens standing in the doorway of the breakroom. She knew from the stern expression on his face and the fact that he'd used her title instead of her first name that he did not have good news, but she'd been expecting his visit. She'd known when she made the video a few days ago that retribution would come for her. She just hadn't known when.

"Yes, sir." She was determined to stand strong. She'd done nothing wrong. The government and the media had perpetrated this awful event on the people and she'd been complicit for too long. She would not apologize for speaking up now.

She followed him to his office and waited as he shut the door and crossed to his desk.

"Sit down," he said, pointing to the chair.

Candace sat and folded her hands in her lap.

"You have created quite the problem for us, Dr. Markham," Dr. Aikens said, steepling his hands together underneath his jowly chin.

Candace said nothing as she waited for him to continue.

"I'm sure you understand what I am referring to," Dr. Aikens continued. When Candace merely lifted an eyebrow, he continued, "Your video has gotten quite a few views and now people are looking into this hospital."

"Perhaps they should be," Candace said, "What we've been doing is wrong."

Anger flashed in Dr. Aikens's eyes. "We have done nothing illegal. We've simply benefitted from the government's incentives."

"At the expense of fear and panic of the public. People are suffering mentally from the isolation. Did you know that suicide and homicide numbers are through the roof? People are dying from things other than NVAC because they're too scared to come in and get checked out. And don't you care why the government offered those incentives? Don't you wonder why they wanted the numbers to seem much higher than they are?"

"That is not our concern," Dr. Aikens said with a shrug.

"Perhaps it should be." Candace leaned forward and placed her hands on the edge of Dr. Aikens's desk. "We've been told to inflate the numbers and we did. Now we are being told to push this vaccine and we are, but have you looked into this vaccine? Have you gone down and checked in on Anne who shakes so uncontrollably that she can barely function now after taking this vaccine? Or how about the five people who died in the ER last week after receiving the vaccine? Have you looked into them? Have you researched Daman Caturix? Because I have. The man stated that the way to lower population growth was with good vaccines. Good vaccines, Dr. Aikens? He's talking about vaccines killing people to slow the population growth. The same vaccines we are telling people are safe to take."

"I don't believe he actually said that," Dr. Aikens said, sitting back.

"You can look it up for yourself. It was a video of him speaking."

"Look, regardless of what he once said, you have a choice to make. You can either take the vaccine and release a video telling the world you were wrong and it is safe or you can find another job."

Candace knew this day would come. She had hoped it wouldn't come this soon, but she'd been prepared for it. "I will not continue to lie to people and be responsible for their deaths. I pray for your soul."

She stood and left the room before he could say anything else. There was only one thing she needed to do before she left the hospital.

Anne's body was still convulsing when she entered the room, but the woman flashed a hopeful smile at Candace. "Do you have any good news?"

"I don't yet, Anne," Candace said, picking up the woman's trembling hand. "I just got fired and I'm moving to Olympia to work with some people down there. I can't guarantee we'll be able to help you any better, but will you come with me?"

Anne blinked at her. "Do you think they will be able to help me here?"

"I don't know." Candace wished she could assure her friend, but she didn't want to give false hope. "They definitely have more equipment here than I'll have access to down there, but I can't in good faith say this hospital has their patients' best interest at heart. What I can tell you is that where I'm going, the people will try. They will research and not stop until they find a cure for you."

Anne chewed on her bottom lip for a moment. "Then I'm coming with you."

"Seriously, Katie, what is going on?" Lily asked as they looked out at the half-empty cafeteria. It had been a week since their run-in with Mr. Dagon, and while they'd managed to avoid him outside of class, they could no longer deny that the population of the school had taken a serious hit.

Katie glanced around and answered in a hushed voice, "I don't know, but a few students are saying that some got the vaccine and are home sick because of it."

"Well, that goes against their narrative that the vaccine was supposed to keep people from getting sick," Lily said as she unwrapped her sandwich. "No wonder they're not sharing that news."

"Yeah, but what does that mean for us, Lily? I know there are a few others who are going to refuse to take it, but how long do you think we really have before they start pressuring us?"

"My guess is not long." Lily tried to force a smile, but inside she fought an overwhelming sense of sadness. She'd wanted this year to be different, to be normal, but she was very afraid that nothing would ever be normal again.

"Help, someone help!"

Lily and Katie jumped from their seats and raced over to the girl shouting for help. She was younger, probably a freshman as Lily didn't recognize her, and she was bending over a boy who appeared to have fallen out of his seat. The boy was also unfamiliar to Lily.

"What happened?" Lily asked as she pulled out her phone and dialed 9-1-1.

"I don't know," the girl said. "He was eating and then he just grabbed his chest and fell over."

"9-1-1, what's your emergency?" the woman on the other end of the phone asked.

"There's a boy here who passed out or something," Lily said. "He was eating lunch and then he grabbed his chest and fell over."

"Is he breathing?" the woman asked.

Lily looked to Katie. "She wants to know if he's breathing."

Katie placed her hand over the boy's mouth and nodded. "He is but just barely."

"I told him he shouldn't have done it," the girl said, sobbing as she wrapped her arms around her knees.

"What's your location?" the woman in Lily's ear asked.

"What did he do?" Katie placed a hand on the girl's shoulder in an effort to calm her down.

The girl lifted her head, her eyes brimming with liquid. "He took the vaccine."

"Ma'am, are you there? I need to verify your location," the woman said in Lily's ear.

"Uh, Mountain Elm High School," Lily said into the phone, trying to concentrate on both conversations.

"Please stay on the line. We're sending help."

Katie caught her eyes before looking back to the girl. "Are you saying you think the vaccine caused this?"

"I'm not crazy," she said, shaking her head. "I've done my research."

"We don't think you're crazy," Katie said. "We believe you."

"What is the meaning of this? You are all breaking the six-foot distance rule."

Lily looked up to see Mr. Dagon coming their direction.

"I've got this," Katie said, standing and meeting the teacher before he could reach them. "A boy collapsed. We've called 9-1-1, and we will wait with him until they get here."

"You called 9-1-1? That is not policy."

"Not policy?" Katie's voice rose in anger. "Since when? The boy collapsed. Calling for an ambulance should *always* be the first priority." Katie placed her hands on her hips and though Lily could not see her face, she could imagine the glare emanating from her eyes. Her friend might have a soft exterior but she was fierce on the inside if backed into a corner.

Mr. Dagon folded his arms across his chest and returned her stare, but before he could say anything more, Mr. Shane and Mrs. Fox rushed in.

"What happened?" Mrs. Fox asked as she knelt down beside Lily.

Lily pointed to the girl. She didn't know the girl's name and felt bad as she realized she should have asked. "She was with him, but she said he grabbed his chest and collapsed. I've got 9-1-1 on the line."

The sound of a siren cut through the air and moments later, two paramedics rushed in and took over. Lily took a step back and found Katie. Mr. Dagon, it seemed, had disappeared.

Candace parked the car and walked around to help Anne out. Her husband Stanley climbed out of the passenger side and came over to help as well.

"Are you sure this is the place?" he asked, eyeing the small house.

"It probably won't be the final place, but yes, I have friends inside and we can stay here until we find a more permanent place."

They each took one of Anne's arms and helped her up the steps. Candace entered the key code Raven had sent her into the box and pushed the door open.

"Hello," she called as they entered, "Raven? You here?"

"She ran for some groceries," a male voice from the direction of the kitchen said. A moment later, the owner of the voice appeared. Though she'd never met him,

Candace assumed this had to be Gabe Cross, and she was surprised to find her breath catch just a little when she saw him.

"Hi, I'm Candace Markham and this is Anne and Stanley-"

"Oh, right, here let me help." He hurried toward them, but stopped short as if trying to decide the best way to help. "Raven told me you were coming. We've got a room prepared for you, Anne. Follow me. I'm Gabe Cross, by the way," he said as he led the way toward the bedrooms. "Sorry, I should have introduced myself earlier."

"It's fine," Candace said. "We're just happy you have a place for us."

"Yeah, unfortunately, this house is getting a little small. We'll probably be moving to the shelter soon, but we'll make sure everything is set up for you there as well."

Anne nodded. "Thank you," she said as they helped her into the bed. "It means so much to me."

"To us," Stanley said, grabbing her hand. He turned to Gabe. "We don't have kids anymore. They were taken in the disappearances. I'm in decent health, but I'm not sure the best way to help her. I have to admit I was afraid of letting her leave the hospital."

Candace placed a comforting hand on his shoulder. She knew this decision hadn't been easy for him. It hadn't been that easy for her either, leaving almost everything she owned back in Seattle. "Don't worry, Stanley. I promise I will be here even if I have to sleep on the couch."

"And I've been researching some remedies," Gabe said. "Experimental, but safe, so if you're open to trying them-"

"I'll try anything," Anne said. "Anything to get my life back. However much longer we have."

"You only took the first shot, right?" Gabe asked.

"That's right. She lost control shortly after and was never able to get the second."

"That's actually good news," Gabe said, smiling at Stanley and Anne. "It means there are fewer mRNA cells in your body, and we may be able to fight what's there. We're going to start with a healthy diet of only natural foods, nothing processed. Then we'll add in Coconut and Red Palm Oil, Turmeric, and Vitamin D and E."

"And that will work?" The hope in Stanley's voice tore at Candace's heart.

"It will certainly help," Gabe said with a nod. "Our bodies want natural foods, and it's amazing how much we can heal ourselves with the right nutrients. Now, how about you two get settled and Dr. Markham and I will go and get the rest of your things?"

"Thank you." They were only two words, but Candace could see the relief on Anne's face and the tiny tear that trickled out of the corner of her eye.

"That was great what you said in there," Candace said

when they reached the living room. "I didn't know you were researching a cure for her."

"Well, it's not like I have much else to do now that I'm out of work. Plenty of time to research."

"I guess that's one benefit then. Does it get easier? Not working? Because it's only been a few days and I'm going crazy."

Gabe flashed her a small smile. "A little, but maybe it will be easier with a partner in crime."

"A partner in crime?" Candace said with a laugh. "I like that. I never thought of myself as being a criminal, but I guess when you stand on the right side, on God's side, sometimes the world will see you that way."

A light pink crossed Gabe's cheeks, and he nodded before opening the door for her.

"If I could have everyone's attention." The intercom crackled as Mr. Shane's voice came over the loudspeaker. "I'm sorry for the interruption, but I have some important information." He paused as if gathering his courage. "The first is that we have been informed that Bradley King, the student who collapsed the other day, has passed away. Unfortunately, due to NCAV restrictions, we are unable to attend a funeral for him, but we will post on the website ways to help out his family for those who are interested."

A collective gasp went up across the room, and Lily glanced at Katie. Though neither of them had wanted this outcome, they had suspected it might be coming. In her latest video, Raven had shared how many people had died after receiving the vaccine - a number that no one else was talking about.

"In addition, we have learned that several of your fellow students are in the hospital. Because of this, we will be canceling in-person school for the rest of the semester and finishing online. I know that is not what you hoped when you joined us this year, but my hope is that by next semester, we will have everyone vaccinated and be able to return."

Everyone vaccinated? Didn't they realize Bradley's death was due to the vaccine? Lily thought. There was no way everyone would get vaccinated.

"Please come and see me if you have any questions. We will grant one hour for you to gather up all your supplies, but then it is important that you leave campus."

Lily glanced to Mrs. Fox as Mr. Shane ended his speech. Fear and dismay swam in her normally warm gaze. "Mrs. Fox?" Lily asked, raising her hand.

The students around her quieted down as Mrs. Fox wiped the corner of her eye. "Yes, Lily?"

"Will they let us return if we don't get vaccinated?"

"Yeah, I want to know that too because I heard Bradley died from a heart attack caused by the vaccine," a boy in the back added.

"From what I've been told, the answer is no," Mrs. Fox said, her voice marred with sadness. "The governor is pushing for mandatory vaccinations by the end of the year, so it is with a heavy heart that I tell you I won't be returning either."

A chorus of confusion broke out in the room with students shouting, "What?" "No!" "You can't!"

Lily didn't know why, but suddenly she felt God telling her to speak. She stood up in her chair and held her hands up. When everyone quieted down, she took a deep breath. "I don't know how many of you lost someone in the disappearances, and I don't know what you believe about what caused them, but I believe it was the rapture. That means we are now in the tribulation period and things are only going to get worse. I know this is scary, but I belong to a group called TruthSeekers. You can find them online. Look them up, watch what they say, think for yourself, and if you think I'm right, they'll tell you how to find us."

For a moment there was silence as the room stared at her with wide eyes and open mouths. Then suddenly, the flood gates opened, and the room began peppering her with questions. The corners of Lily's mouth curled into a soft smile. Raven had been right. They might not save everyone, but many were looking for hope and truth.

Raven pulled her mask on as she approached the entrance of the store. She wished she could be like some of the believers she saw in more conservative states and just refuse to wear it, but here she would be refused service. And for now at least, it was important that she get supplies.

She slowed though as the door opened, revealing a guard of some sort standing just inside. He held only a clipboard, but that did not put Raven at ease. *What was going on?*

"Have you been vaccinated, Miss?" he asked as she stepped through the door.

"How is that any of your business?"

"I'm sorry, Miss, I'm just following orders. I was told to ask everyone who entered a few simple questions. We're taking no personal data if that makes you feel better."

It didn't. "What happens if I refuse?" Raven asked. She would go to another store if she had to, but she had a sinking feeling that even if they weren't like this one today, they would be soon.

"Then I'm afraid I can't let you enter."

"Are you kidding me? First, you asked for fifteen days, then you asked for face coverings, then double masks, now vaccines and questions?" A few people nearby turned at her raised voice.

"I'm sorry, Miss, I really am."

The man shrugged, and Raven sighed. He probably was just doing his job. He was a sheep, doing what the government told him, but it wasn't his fault really. He had probably never been woken up. "Fine, I'll answer your questions on one condition."

His brow furrowed, but his curiosity won out. "What is that?"

"You check out my website. That's all. Look it up, watch a few videos. You do that, and I promise I'll answer your questions and make no further disturbance."

The man seemed confused, but he agreed, taking the card she held out to him and placing it in his pocket.

"No, I have not been vaccinated," Raven said, answering his original question.

He marked something on his clipboard. "Do you plan to be?"

"No, I do not."

With a nod, he marked again. "I am required to now tell you that this store, come the first of the year, will no longer allow entry to someone who has not been vaccinated."

Raven had known this was coming, but this timeline was only a few months away. "And how exactly will you know if I've been vaccinated? I don't see them handing out papers when you get one, and I'm not walking around with my vaccination record."

"That won't be necessary, Miss. We'll be able to scan your arm with a blacklight and see the vaccine markers."

"I see. Well, thanks for the warning. After today, I'll be sure to take my business elsewhere." As Raven grabbed a cart and began loading it up, her mind played back over the public vaccinations they'd seen and the ingredient list she'd looked at both from Lily and later online as she researched. Neither had listed Luciferase. So were they lying to the public and deliberately failing to mention it? She wouldn't put that past the government or Daman Caturix at least.

She paused to grab vitamins and first aid supplies from the shelf and that's when it hit her. The Band-aids. Caturix's initial patent had been for an implant system - a patch that people could apply themselves. What if he'd put his implant system on the Band-aids they were giving people after the injection? It would be a way for them to inject people with Luciferase without anyone raising concern over it being in the vaccine. But how would he get the infected Band-aids to them and how would he know which people would be giving out the shots? Unless...

A sick feeling settled in the bottom of her stomach as she examined the box of Band-aids in her hand. What if every Band-aid was infected with his implantation system? It would be the only way to be sure all the people who received vaccines also got the Luciferase, but it would also be a way to sneak it into people who refused the vaccine.

She grabbed a few boxes and threw them into the cart. Gabe would be able to determine if they contained the luminescent along with anything else. She just hoped that if she was right, she would have time to warn everyone before it was too late.

20

Raven took a deep breath as she stared at the camera. This was probably the hardest message she'd had to deliver so far.

"My fellow TruthSeekers, I hope this video finds you well. As I'm sure many of you have heard, the government is pushing for a vaccine mandate to be put in place by the end of the year. This means that you will not be able to shop, work, or travel if you do not have the vaccine. For many of you, I know this is a scary time. We were told these tribulation years would not be easy. My hope is that you have a TruthSeeker organization near you. We are working together to build communes for people to live in when they can no longer live in their houses. We are growing our own gardens and some of our organizations are raising animals to help supply food as well. That does not mean this will be easy, but with God's help, we will get through it together.

She paused. Now came the hard part. "Unfortunately, we have discovered something that is of vital importance to share with you. As you will remember, Gabe Cross and I presented about Daman Caturix and his implantation system. We did not see Luciferase listed as an ingredient in the vaccine, so we were puzzled how they were going to be able to check for vaccination. It appears that Caturix has infected all Band-aids. Those receiving the shot are receiving the Luciferase when they get their Band-aid and they don't even know it. Unfortunately, they are also receiving a second dose of the vaccine which is probably why we are seeing so many adverse effects. I know most of you are avoiding the vaccine as we are, but the real problem is that all the Band-aids are infected, so if you use one, you are unknowingly receiving the vaccine. It is important that you immediately stop using Band-aids and find other ways to cover cuts.

"We are working on a way to imitate the Luciferase so that we can still shop, but we are not there yet. Above all, we want to make sure that whatever we do is safe. Please continue to pray, share the truth, and keep your head up. The worst is yet to come, but it will come and what will meet us on the other side will be a much brighter future. I love you all and hope that someday we can meet face to face. God Bless."

Raven ended the video and sat back in the chair. For the first time in months, she wished Kat were here. She wished she could bounce ideas off her and make sure she was on the right track. It was stressful being the face of the resistance, and above all, she wanted to make sure she wasn't leading people astray.

"This was your destiny."

Raven turned to see Kat standing behind her. "Kat?" She jumped from the chair and rushed to the girl. "Is that really you?"

Kat smiled softly. "I'm not physically here with you, but God knew that you needed comfort and assurance."

"Kat, I wish you were really here. I don't know if I'm cut out to be a leader. Sure, I can talk to all these people on the video, but what happens when it comes time and we can't shop or work? What am I going to do to help all these people?"

"The same thing you are doing now. Giving them hope. Do you think you are alone, Raven?"

"No, obviously I have the TruthSeekers here, but what about the rest of the state, the rest of the world?"

Kat's smile widened. "They have their own Ravens. God made sure that people like you would be in the right places to lead and protect the people. Did you think He didn't have a plan?"

Raven bit her lip. As much as she'd grown in her relationship with God, she supposed she had forgotten that He was in control. "So, I can't mess it up?"

"Not if you trust Him. Remember to pray about everything. Continue to build each other up and stay strong. This will be hard, but it will not be forever."

"Will we all make it? To the end?" Raven wasn't sure she actually wanted to hear the answer.

"That is not for me to tell." Kat glanced up and then smiled once more at Raven. "I have to go, but remember to pray."

Raven watched Kat shimmer and disappear in front of her eyes, but the only emotion she felt was relief. "Thank you, God," she said, looking up at the ceiling. "Thank you."

A knock sounded at the door, and a moment later, Gabe poked his head in. "If you're done recording, you might want to come out here."

Raven nodded and uploaded the video to the website before following Gabe.

Anne, who was improving every day with Gabe's treatment, sat in one of the recliners. Her body still convulsed but the tremors were slower and the time between them grew each day. Stanley sat in one of the dining chairs he had pulled up next to her. He held her hand in his. Candace sat on the couch, and all three faced the television.

"This is it, isn't it?" Candace asked as the breaking

news banner flashed across the screen before Governor Smythe's face filled it. The tension in the room was thick.

"Good afternoon. I come to you today to tell you that while our numbers are going down, they are not falling as quickly as we'd hoped. I know we originally stated that we would not require the vaccine in Washington state, but it is our hope that by mandating this vaccine, we can finally get back to a new normal," Governor Smythe said as he smiled out at the camera.

"I wish I could punch him," Candace said as her hand balled into fists. "I wish I could wipe that smile off his face and demand that he be held accountable for all the deaths he caused this year with his lockdowns, his mask mandates, and now his pushing of the dangerous vaccine."

"We all do," Gabe said, placing a calming hand on her arm. "But that's not our place."

"That's right," Anne said. "Justice belongs to God, and He will take it."

"Stations will be set up at every store and business across Washington state and will be manned every hour the store is open," the Governor continued. "Customers will be scanned with a blacklight, allowing us to see your vaccine documentation. Those without documentation will not be admitted. It is my hope that all of you will choose to do this small sacrifice for the greater good. Vaccine stations will be set up at all hospitals and pharmacies. While it will take some time to get all of this up and running across the state, this order will go into effect next week, so please do not delay in getting your vaccine. That is all."

The governor did not take any questions, but it didn't matter. He wouldn't have answered the only one that mattered anyway.

Candace turned off the TV and the group sat in silence for a moment. "I guess it's time then," Candace finally said.

They all knew what she meant. They'd been preparing for it for months, but it didn't make it any easier. Living in the warehouse, no matter how nicely Nathan and the others had fixed it up, wouldn't be the same as living in their own houses or living here for that matter. But it would be safer. And right now, that was what mattered the most.

"We have a few days, maybe even a couple of weeks," Raven said, "but I agree, we should start moving anything over we're going to need. Obviously, space will be small, so let's only take that which will be necessary."

"Thankfully, Stan and I left most of our stuff up in Seattle anyway," Anne said with a soft laugh.

"As did I," Candace said. "After all, those things were just things."

"Agreed," Gabe said. "To be honest, I think I might

even be happier with less stuff. There's definitely less to clean."

Raven knew he was trying to lighten the mood, and she appreciated it. She glanced around at her small circle of friends and smiled when she realized these people weren't even half of the group she now called friends. The future might be unknown, but she knew that whatever happened, they could make it through together.

The End!

Want to find out what happens to Raven and the rest? Be sure to preorder Faith Over Fear now

Also, if you liked this book, please leave a review. Just a few words really helps!

IT'S NOT QUITE THE END!

Thank you so much for reading *The Beginning of the End!* This book started so differently that it's interesting to me to see how much it changed. I promised that I would provide links to things I discussed in here, and so I will, but before I do, I want to say that I hoped you enjoyed this story. If you did, would you do me a favor? Please leave a review at your retailer. It really helps. It doesn't have to be long - just a few words to help other readers know what they're getting.

I'd love to hear from you, not only about this story, but about the characters or stories you'd like read in the future. I'm always looking for new ideas and if I use one of your characters or stories, I'll send you a free ebook and paperback of the book with a special dedication. Write to me at loranahoopes@gmail.com. And if you'd like to see what's coming next, be sure to stop by authorloranahoopes.org

I also have a weekly newsletter that contains many wonderful things like pictures of my adorable children, chances to win awesome prizes, new releases and sales I might be holding, great books from other authors, and anything else that strikes my fancy and that I think you would enjoy. I'll even send you the first chapter of my newest (maybe not even released yet) book if you'd like to sign up.

Even better, I solemnly swear to only send out one newsletter a week (usually on Tuesday unless life gets in the way which with three kids it usually does). I will not spam you, sell your email address to solicitors or anyone else, or any of those other terrible things.

Here are the links so you can do your own digging. As I tell my students, there are two sides to every story and every story is biased. So look at both because somewhere in the middle is the truth. Remember, trust the still small voice that you hear.

https://stateofthenation.co/?p=30117

https://www.photonics.com/Articles/

Quantum_Dots_Deliver_Vaccines_Encode_Vaccination/a65443

https://www.exposingsatanism.org/luciferase-the-micro-needle-vaccine-delivery-system/

https://www.americasfrontlinedoctors.com/

https://www.centerforhealthsecurity.org/event201/about

https://vaxpain.us/

https://www.afa.net/the-stand/culture/2020/09/it-is-scientifically-impossible-for-masks-to-work/

https://www.rcreader.com/commentary/masks-dont-work-covid-a-review-of-science-relevant-to-covide-19-social-policy

https://principia-scientific.com/covid-19-masks-causing-rise-in-bacterial-pneumonia/

https://www.nih.gov/news-events/news-releases/bacterial-pneumonia-caused-most-deaths-1918-influenza-pandemic

https://nypost.com/2020/04/29/dr-fauci-backed-controversial-wuhan-lab-studying-coronavirus/

https://www.youtube.com/watch?v=PAJ3YhlUegk

https://www.instagram.com/tv/CLR9r_ugFFH/?utm_source=ig_web_button_share_sheet&fbclid=IwAR2yjOPzLCW5HNsLD6OhezMWZ8JHdVvtboRgvC82zHT8AVZfdVUxSu4cQYU

https://www.lifesitenews.com/news/mrna-covid-19-vaccines-are-really-gene-therapy-and-not-vaccines-ethicist

https://sandrarose.com/2020/12/fda-releases-list-of-
mrna-vaccine-side-effects/

https://www.lifesavinghealth.org/parkinsons-disease-
natural-cures-treatments-remedies.html

https://www.msn.com/en-us/health/medical/whats-
in-the-covid-19-vaccines-we-asked-experts-to-explain-the-
ingredients/ar-BB1c12ow

https://www.drugs.com/sfx/potassium-phosphate-
side-effects.html

https://l.facebook.com/l.php?u=https%3A%2F%
2Fwww.globalresearch.ca%2Flong-term-mask-use-may-
contribute-advanced-stage-lung-cancer-study-finds%
2F5736339%3Ffbclid%
3DIwAR0m2rXipsgZGXDdMla_IvJ7SFLOjnSUjAJyySx
6GiE4-ugiQzL3bd8TT5U&h=
AT0QncXj5DMac1Y6OoPJGPnn23YeKAuDJbP_5ZpKs
gsLZN_hG3Wvhd6E8gFIGlJstGc9s3dj6Bc2q-
lgsh4Og1LHHsjUDziXIvEWeoZxxNl99VmDlEjkiPIQh
Q5F_QXSWu4yWVUoJpfm1g_LrLEuQP8&__tn__=-
UK-R&c

https://www.globalresearch.ca/long-term-mask-use-
may-contribute-advanced-stage-lung-cancer-study-finds/
5736339?fbclid=
IwAR0m2rXipsgZGXDdMla_IvJ7SFLOjnSUjAJyySx6Gi
E4-ugiQzL3bd8TT5U

https://rumble.com/vcyy1v-dr.-david-martin-warns-
this-is-not-a-vaccine.html?

fbclid=IwAR07jThu9n_RZYCKdCZvFEQpUbXdhnXC ggTvJQj8UkQOVc__RJAvDx91MLI

https://principia-scientific.com/covid-deaths-75percent-lower-in-nations-using-hcq/?fbclid=IwAR3z9fMZ4IGTbKfXHLRMHjLmLnuo9WhcTWtikU9bt7icjUHly8nq5JQYB-I

21
A FREE STORY FOR YOU

Enjoyed this story? Not ready to quit reading yet? If you sign up for my newsletter, you will receive The Billionaire's Impromptu Bet right away as my thank you gift for choosing to hang out with me.

The Billionaire's Impromptu Bet

A SWAT officer. A bored billionaire heiress. A bet that could change everything....

Read on for a taste of The Billionaire's Impromptu Bet....

22
THE BILLIONAIRE'S IMPROMPTU BET PREVIEW

Brie Carter fell back spread eagle on her queen-sized canopy bed sending her blonde hair fanning out behind her. With a large sigh, she uttered, "I'm bored."

"How can you be bored? You have like millions of dollars." Her friend, Ariel, plopped down in a seated position on the bed beside her and flicked her raven hair off her shoulder. "You want to go shopping? I hear Tiffany's is having a special right now."

Brie rolled her eyes. Shopping? Where was the excitement in that? With her three platinum cards, she could go shopping whenever she wanted. "No, I'm bored with shopping too. I have everything. I want to do something exciting. Something we don't normally do."

Brie enjoyed being rich. She loved the unlimited credit

cards at her disposal, the constant apparel of new clothes, and of course the penthouse apartment her father paid for, but lately, she longed for something more fulfilling.

Ariel's hazel eyes widened. "I know. There's a new bar down on Franklin Street. Why don't we go play a little game?"

Brie sat up, intrigued at the secrecy and the twinkle in Ariel's eyes. "What kind of game?"

"A betting game. You let me pick out any man in the place. Then you try to get him to propose to you."

Brie wrinkled her nose. "But I don't want to get married." She loved her freedom and didn't want to share her penthouse with anyone, especially some man.

"You don't marry him, silly. You just get him to propose."

Brie bit her lip as she thought. It had been awhile since her last relationship and having a man dote on her for a month might be interesting, but.... "I don't know. It doesn't seem very nice."

"How about I sweeten the pot? If you win, I'll set you up on a date with my brother."

Brie cocked her head. Was she serious? The only thing Brie couldn't seem to buy in the world was the affection of Ariel's very handsome, very wealthy, brother. He was a movie star, just the kind of person Brie could consider marrying in the future. She'd had a crush on him as long as she and Ariel had been friends, but he'd always seen her as just that, his little sister's friend. "I thought you didn't want me dating your brother."

"I don't." Ariel shrugged. "But he's between girlfriends right now, and I know you've wanted it for ages. If you win this bet, I'll set you up. I can't guarantee any more than one date though. The rest will be up to you."

Brie wasn't worried about that. Charm she possessed in abundance. She simply needed some alone time with him, and she was certain she'd be able to convince him they were meant to be together. "All right. You've got a deal."

Ariel smiled. "Perfect. Let's get you changed then and see who the lucky man will be.

A tiny tug pulled on Brie's heart that this still wasn't right, but she dismissed it. This was simply a means to an end, and he'd never have to know.

Jesse Calhoun relaxed as the rhythmic thudding of the speed bag reached his ears. Though he loved his job, it was stressful being the SWAT sniper. He hated having to take human lives and today had been especially rough. The team had been called out to a drug bust, and Jesse was forced to return fire at three hostiles. He didn't care that they fired at his team and himself first. Taking a life was always hard, and every one of them haunted his dreams.

"You gonna bust that one too?" His co-worker Brendan appeared by his side. Brendan was the opposite of Jesse in nearly every way. Where Jesse's hair was a dark copper, Brendan's was nearly black. Jesse sported paler skin and a dusting of freckles across his nose, but Brendan's skin was naturally dark and freckle free.

Jesse flashed a crooked grin, but kept his eyes on the small, swinging black bag. The speed bag was his way to release, but a few times he had started hitting while still too keyed up and he had ruptured the bag. Okay, five times, but who was counting really? Besides, it was a better way to calm his nerves than other things he could choose. Drinking, fights, gambling, women.

"Nah, I think this one will last a little longer." His shoulders began to burn, and he gave the bag another few punches for good measure before dropping his arms and letting it swing to a stop. "See? It lives to be hit at least another day." Every once in a while, Jesse missed training the way he used to. Before he joined the force, he had been an amateur boxer, on his way to being a pro, but a shoulder injury had delayed his training and forced him to consider something else. It had eventually healed, but by then he had lost his edge.

"Hey, why don't you come drink with us?" Brendan

clapped a hand on Jesse's shoulder as they headed into the locker room.

"You know I don't drink." Jesse often felt like the outsider of the team. While half of the six-man team was married, the other half found solace in empty bottles and meaningless relationships. Jesse understood that - their job was such that they never knew if they would come home night after night - but he still couldn't partake.

Brendan opened his locker and pulled out a clean shirt. He peeled off his current one and added deodorant before tugging on the new one. "You don't have to drink. Look, I won't drink either. Just come and hang out with us. You have no one waiting for you at home."

That wasn't entirely true. Jesse had Bugsy, his Boston Terrier, but he understood Brendan's point. Most days, Jesse went home, fed Bugsy, made dinner, and fell asleep watching TV on the couch. It wasn't much of a life. "All right, I'll go, but I'm not drinking."

Brendan's lips pulled back to reveal his perfectly white teeth. He bragged about them, but Jesse knew they were veneers. "That's the spirit. Hurry up and change. We don't want to leave the rest of the team waiting."

"Is everyone coming?" Jesse pulled out his shower necessities. Brendan might feel comfortable going out with just a new application of deodorant, but Jesse needed to wash more than just dirt and sweat off. He needed to wash the sound of the bullets and the sight of lifeless bodies from his mind.

"Yeah, Pat's wife is pregnant again and demanding some crazy food concoctions. Pat agreed to pick them up if she let him have an hour. Cam and Jared's wives are having a girls' night, so the whole gang can be together. It will be nice to hang out when we aren't worried about being shot at."

"Fine. Give me ten minutes. Unlike you, I like to clean up before I go out."

Brendan smirked. "I've never had any complaints. Besides, do you know how long it takes me to get my hair like this?"

Jesse shook his head as he walked into the shower, but he knew it was true. Brendan had rugged good looks and muscles to match. He rarely had a hard time finding a woman. Jesse on the other hand hadn't dated anyone in the last few months. It wasn't that he hadn't been looking, but he was quieter than his teammates. And he wasn't looking for right now. He was looking for forever. He just hadn't found it yet.

Click here to continue reading The Billionaire's Impromptu Bet.

THE STORY DOESN'T END!

You've met a few people and fallen in love....

I bet you're wondering how you can meet everyone else.

Star Lake Series:

Sealed with a Kiss: Meet the quirky cast of Star Lake and find out if Max and Layla will ever find love.

When Love Returns: Return to Star Lake to hear Presley's story and find out if she gets the second chance with her first love.

Once Upon a Star: Continue the journey when aspiring actress Audrey returns home with a baby. Will Blake finally get the nerve to share his feelings with her?

Love Conquers All: Meet Lanie Perkins Hall who never imagined being divorced at thirty or falling for an old friend, but will his secrets keep them apart?

e **Star Lake Collection:** Get the latter three stories in one place. Series will include book 1 when it releases around November 2020.

The Heartbeats Series:

Where It All Began: Sandra Baker finds forgiveness and healing even after making a horrible choice.

The Power of Prayer: Will Callie Green find true love or be defined by her mistake?

When Hearts Collide: When Amanda Adams goes to college, she finds a world she was not ready for. But will she also find true love?

A Past Forgiven: Jess Peterson has lived a life of abuse and lost her self worth, but when she finds herself pregnant, will she find new hope?

The Heartbeats Collection: Grab all four Heartbeats novels in one collection

Sweet Billionaires Series:

The Billionaire's Impromptu Bet: Can a spoiled rich girl change when a bet turns to love?

The Billionaire's Secret: Can a playboy settle down when he finds out he has a daughter who needs him?

A Brush with a Billionaire: What happens when a stuck up actor lands in a small town and needs help from a female mechanic?

The Billionaire's Christmas Miracle: A twist on

a Cinderella story when a billionaire meets a woman who doesn't belong at the ball.

The Billionaire's Cowboy Groom: Will one night six years ago keep Carrie from finding true love?

The Cowboy Billionaire: He's there for her land, but he never expected to fall for her.

The Billionaire's Bliss: This collection contains The Billionaire's Secret, The Billionaire's Christmas Miracle, and The Billionaire's Cowboy Groom

The Lawkeeper Series:

Lawfully Matched: When the man she agreed to marry turns out to have a dark past, will Kate have to return home or will she find love with her rescuer in this historical fiction?

Lawfully Justified: Can a bounty hunter and a widow find love together in this historical fiction?

The Scarlet Wedding: William and Emma are planning their wedding, but an outbreak and a return from his past force them to change their plans. Is a happily ever after still in their future in this historical fiction?

Lawfully Redeemed: What happens when a K9 cop falls for the brother of her suspect? Contemporary romance.

The Lawkeeper Collection: Get all four books in one collection

The Are You Listening Series:

The Still Small Voice: Will Jordan listen to God's prompting in this speculative fiction?

A Spark in the Darkness Will Jordan be able to help Raven before the rapture occurs?

The Beginning of the End: After the rapture, Raven is faced with reaching new believers and surviving a pandemic sent to destroy them all.

Faith over Fear coming soon: Forced into hiding, will Rave and the others make it to the end?

Blushing Brides Series:

The Cowboy's Reality Bride: He's agreed to be the bachelor on a reality dating show, but what happens when he falls for a woman who's not one of the contestants?

The Reality Bride's Baby: Laney wants nothing more than a baby, but when she starts feeling dizzy is it pregnancy or something more serious?

The Producer's Unlikely Bride: What happens when a producer and an author agree to a fake relationship?

Ava's Blessing in Disguise: Five years after marriage, Ava faces a mysterious illness that threatens to ruin her career. Will she find out what it is?

The Soldier's Steadfast Bride: Heidi and Cory made a pact as kids. Will she honor it now if it means she might have to marry without love?

The Men of Fire Beach

Fire Games: Cassidy returns home from Who Wants to Marry a Cowboy to find obsessive letters from a fan. The cop assigned to help her wants to get back to his case, but what she sees at a fire may just be the key he's looking for.

Lost Memories and New Beginnings: A doctor, a patient with no memory, the men out to get her. Can he keep her safe when he doesn't know who he's looking for?

When Questions Abound: A Companion story to Lost Memories. Told from Detective Graves' point of view.

Never Forget the Past: Fireman Bubba must confront his past in order to clear his name and save lives.

Love on the Run: Graham is forced into lockdown with one of his employees. Will he be able to save her from her ex and will she steal his heart?

Secrets and Suspense: Cara Hunter is hiding something about her military past. When she's suspected of murder, will she be able to convince Cole she's the victim?

Rescue My Heart coming soon: Al's sister is missing. Can she find her in time?

The Men of Fire Beach Collection: Books 1-3

Texas Tornadoes

Defending My Heart: Forced to confront his past, Emmitt finds news that will change his life.

Run With My Heart: Sentenced to community service, Tucker finds himself falling for the manager.

Love on the Line: Blaine has hired Kenzi to redo his cabin, but what happens when she finds his darkest secret?

Touchdown on Love: When Mason's injury throws him together with ex-girlfriend, will sparks fly again?

Second Chance Reception: Jefferson is hiding something. When he falls for the team cook, will he let her in?

Small Town Short Stories

Small Town Dreams

Small Town Second Chances

Small Town Rivals

Small Town Life

Life in a Small Town: All four stories in one collection

Stand Alones:

Love Renewed: This books is part of the multi author second chance series. When fate reunites high school sweethearts separated by life's choices, can they find a second chance at love at a snowy lodge amid a little mystery?

Her children's early reader chapter book series:

The Wishing Stone #1: Dangerous Dinosaur

The Wishing Stone #2: Dragon Dilemma

The Wishing Stone #3: Mesmerizing Mermaids

The Wishing Stone #4: Pyramid Puzzle
The Wishing Stone: Mary's Miracle
The Wishing Stone #5: Superhero City
The Wishing Stone Collection
To see a list of all her books

authorloranahoopes.com
loranahoopes@gmail.com

ABOUT THE AUTHOR

Lorana Hoopes is an inspirational author originally from Texas but now living in the PNW with her husband and three children. When not writing, she can be seen kick-boxing at the gym, singing, or acting on stage. One day, she hopes to retire from teaching and write full time.

Made in the USA
Middletown, DE
17 April 2021

37864886R00149